HELLO NEIGHBOR™

A GRAPHIC NOVEL

THE SECRET OF BOSCO BAY

BY ZAC GORMAN
ILLUSTRATED BY CHRIS FENOGLIO

SCHOLASTIC INC.

All rights reserved. Published by Graphix, an imprint of Scholastic Inc., *Publishers since 1920*. SCHOLASTIC, GRAPHIX, and associated logos are trademarks and/or registered trademarks of Scholastic Inc.

The publisher does not have any control over and does not assume any responsibility for author or third-party websites or their content.

Library of Congress Control Number Available

ISBN: 978-1-338-66202-3 (hardcover)
ISBN: 978-1-338-59648-9 (paperback)

10 9 8 7 6 5 4 3 2 1   20 21 22 23 24

Printed in the U.S.A.   88
First edition, October 2020
Edited by Michael Petranek and Chloe Fraboni
Art by Chris Fenoglio
Lettering by Bryan Senka
Book design by Heather Daugherty

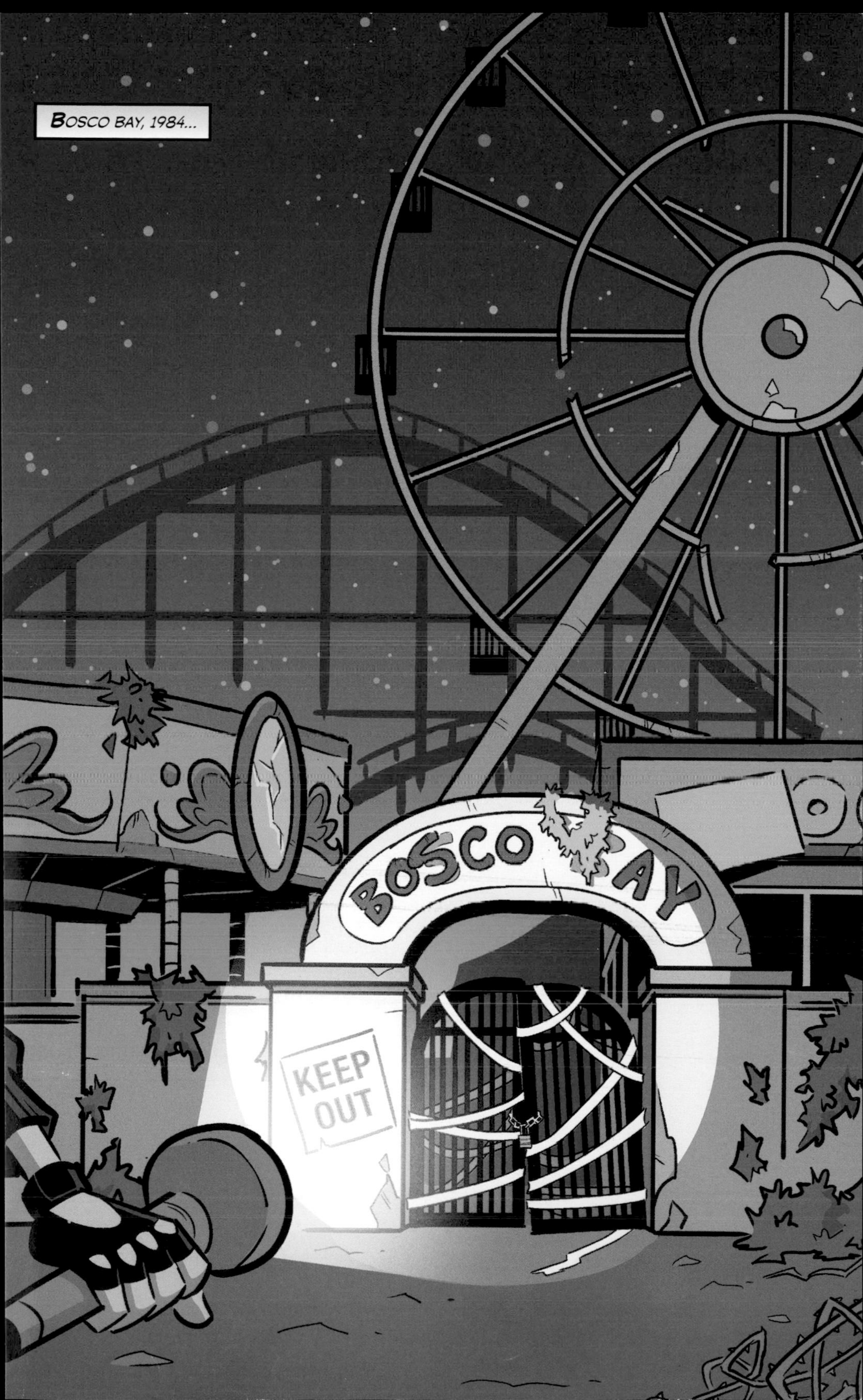

BOSCO BAY, 1984...
BOSCO AY
KEEP OUT

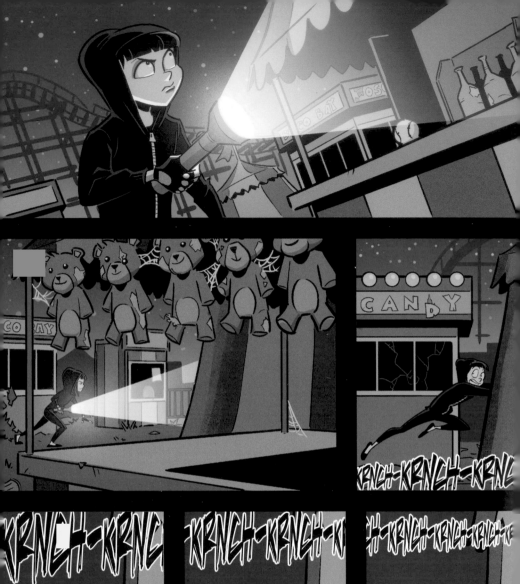

KRNCH-KRNCH-KRNC

KRNCH-KRNC

KRNCH-KRNCH-K

CH-KRNCH KRNCH-KRNCH

hff
hff hff
hff

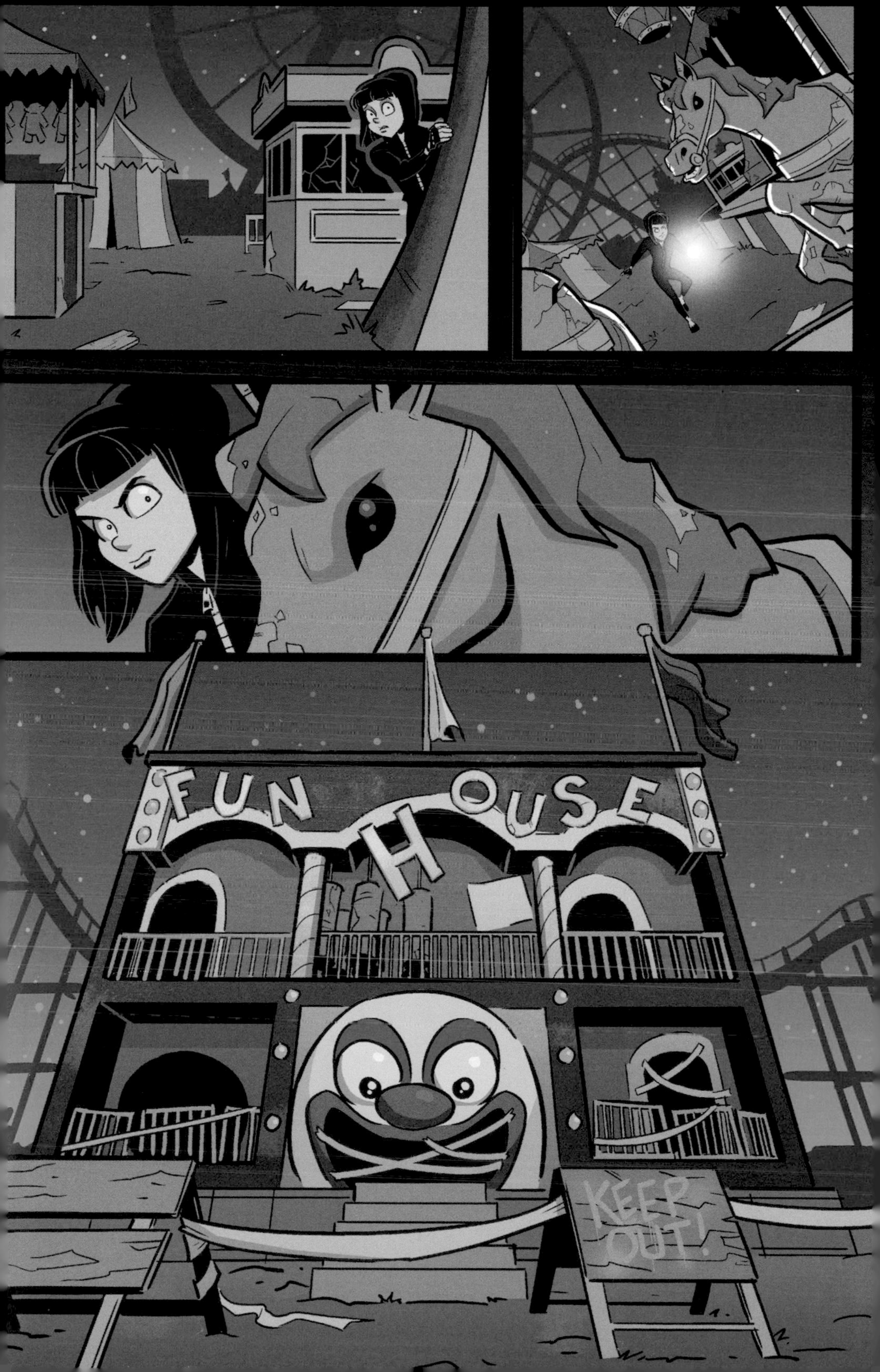
FUN HOUSE
KEEP OUT!

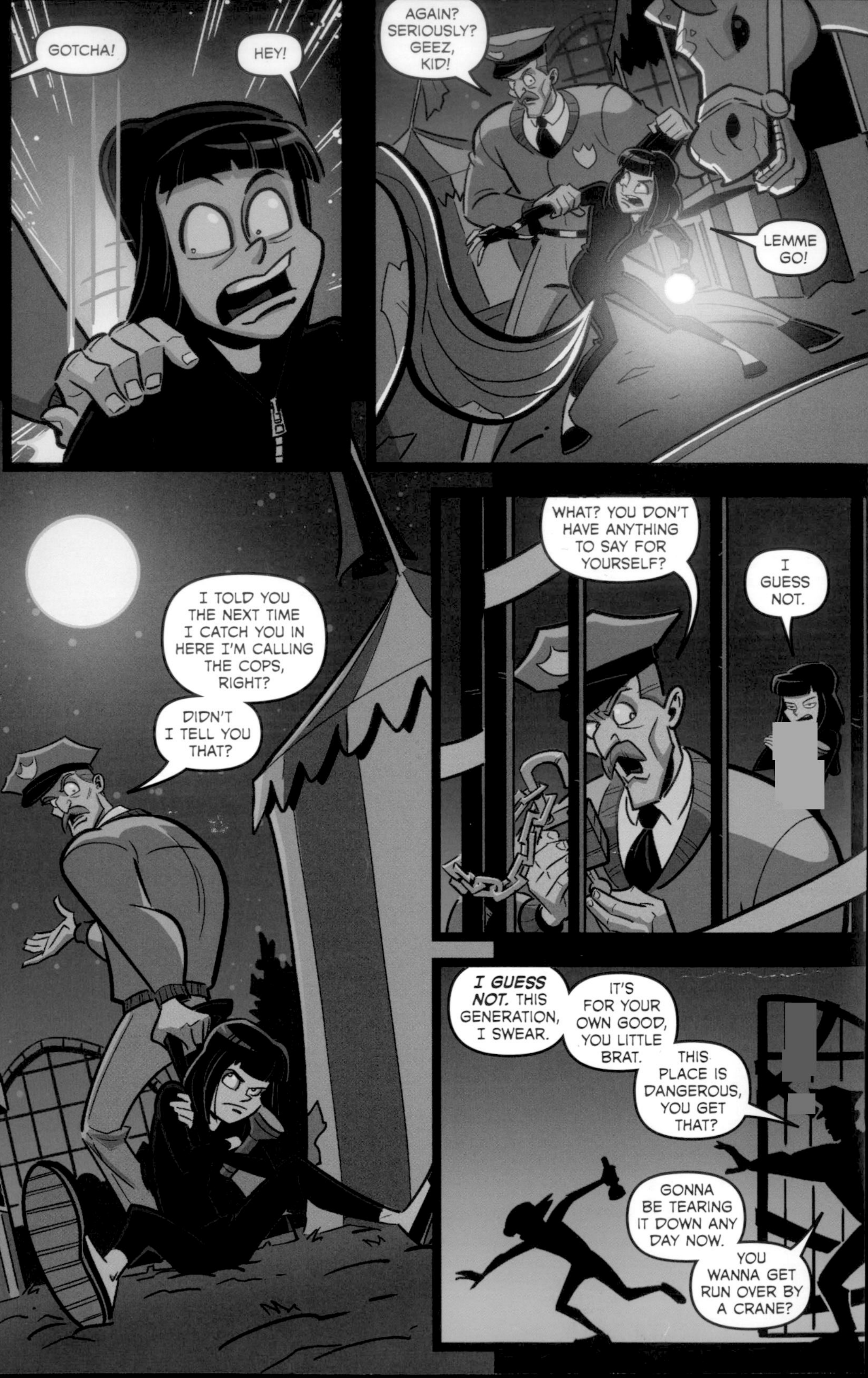
GOTCHA!
HEY!
AGAIN? SERIOUSLY? GEEZ, KID!
LEMME GO!
I TOLD YOU THE NEXT TIME I CATCH YOU IN HERE I'M CALLING THE COPS, RIGHT?
DIDN'T I TELL YOU THAT?
WHAT? YOU DON'T HAVE ANYTHING TO SAY FOR YOURSELF?
I GUESS NOT.
I GUESS NOT. THIS GENERATION, I SWEAR.
IT'S FOR YOUR OWN GOOD, YOU LITTLE BRAT.
THIS PLACE IS DANGEROUS, YOU GET THAT?
GONNA BE TEARING IT DOWN ANY DAY NOW.
YOU WANNA GET RUN OVER BY A CRANE?

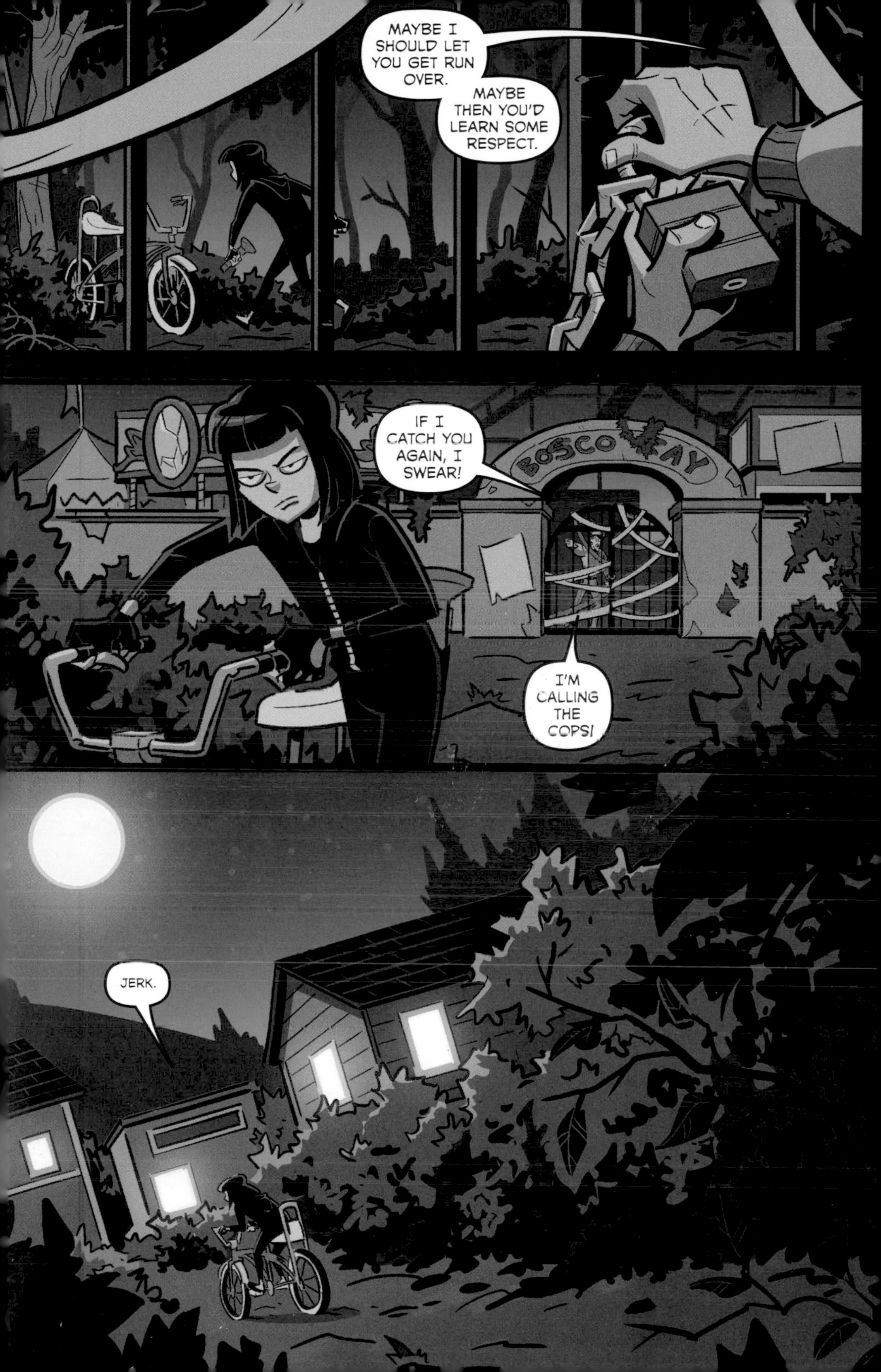
MAYBE I SHOULD LET YOU GET RUN OVER.
MAYBE THEN YOU'D LEARN SOME RESPECT.
BOSCO BAY
IF I CATCH YOU AGAIN, I SWEAR!
I'M CALLING THE COPS!
JERK.

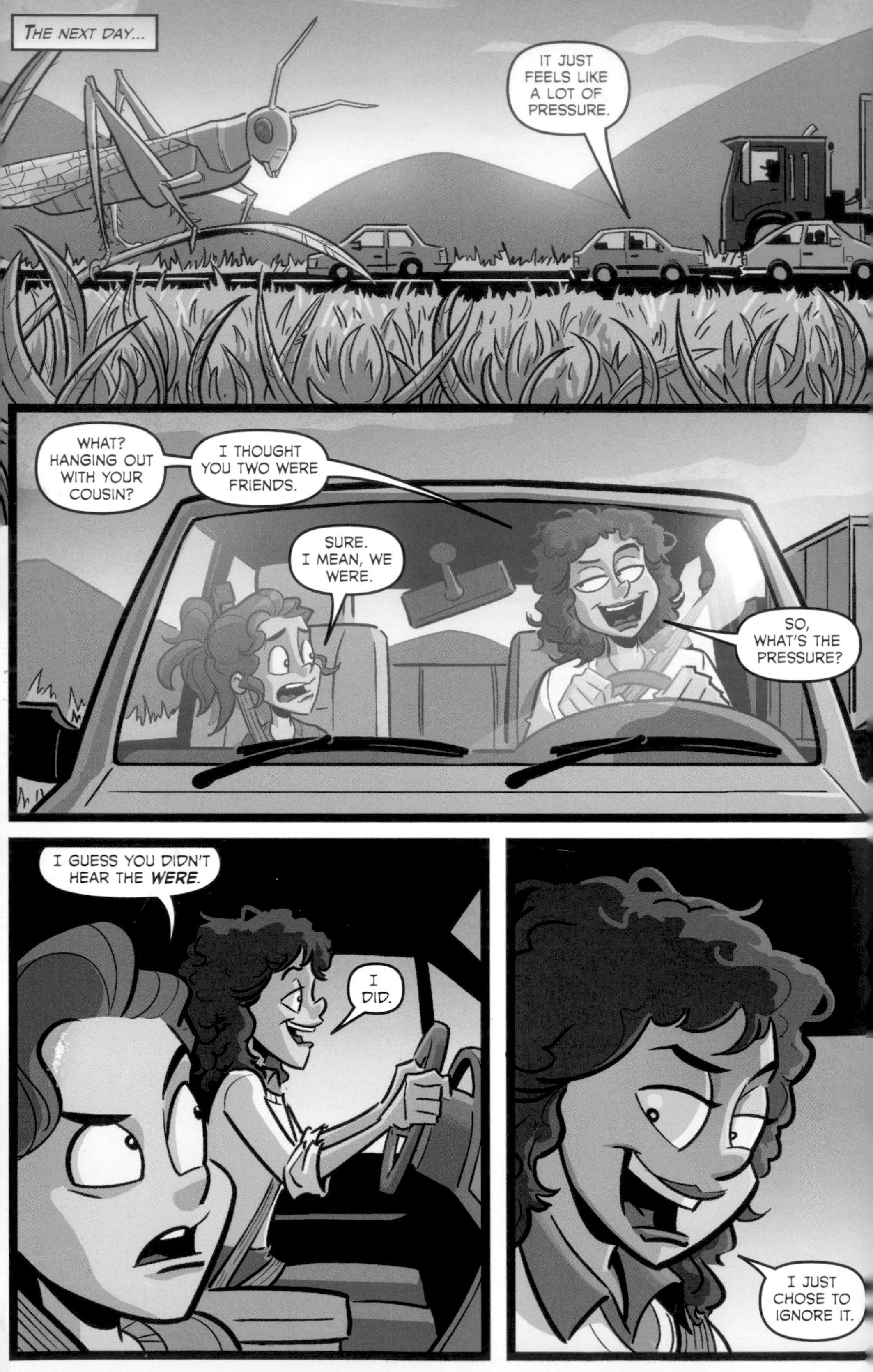
THE NEXT DAY...
IT JUST FEELS LIKE A LOT OF PRESSURE.
WHAT? HANGING OUT WITH YOUR COUSIN?
I THOUGHT YOU TWO WERE FRIENDS.
SURE. I MEAN, WE WERE.
SO, WHAT'S THE PRESSURE?
I GUESS YOU DIDN'T HEAR THE ***WERE***.
I DID.
I JUST CHOSE TO IGNORE IT.

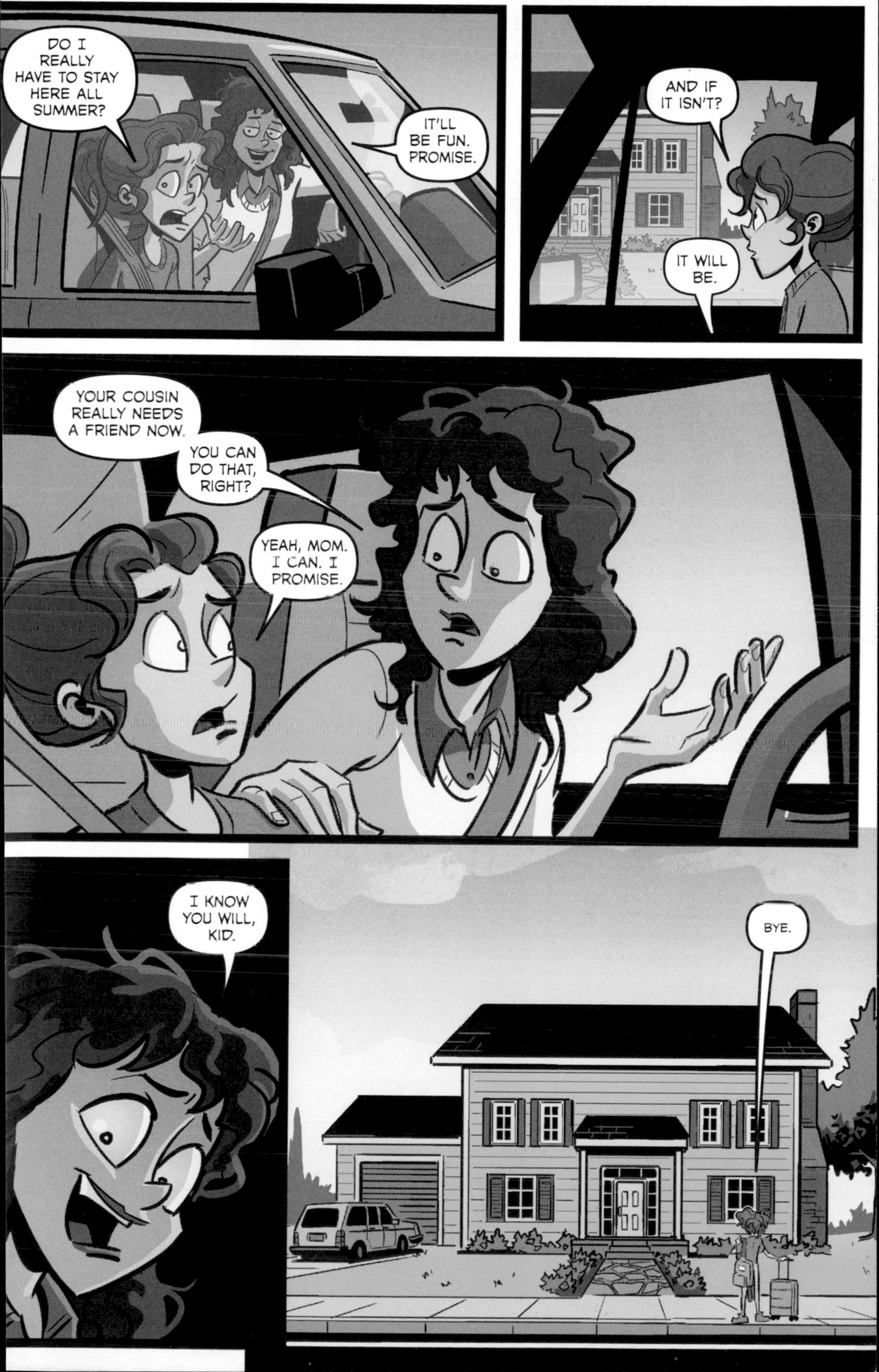
DO I REALLY HAVE TO STAY HERE ALL SUMMER?
IT'LL BE FUN. PROMISE.
AND IF IT ISN'T?
IT WILL BE.
YOUR COUSIN REALLY NEEDS A FRIEND NOW.
YOU CAN DO THAT, RIGHT?
YEAH, MOM. I CAN. I PROMISE.
I KNOW YOU WILL, KID.
BYE.

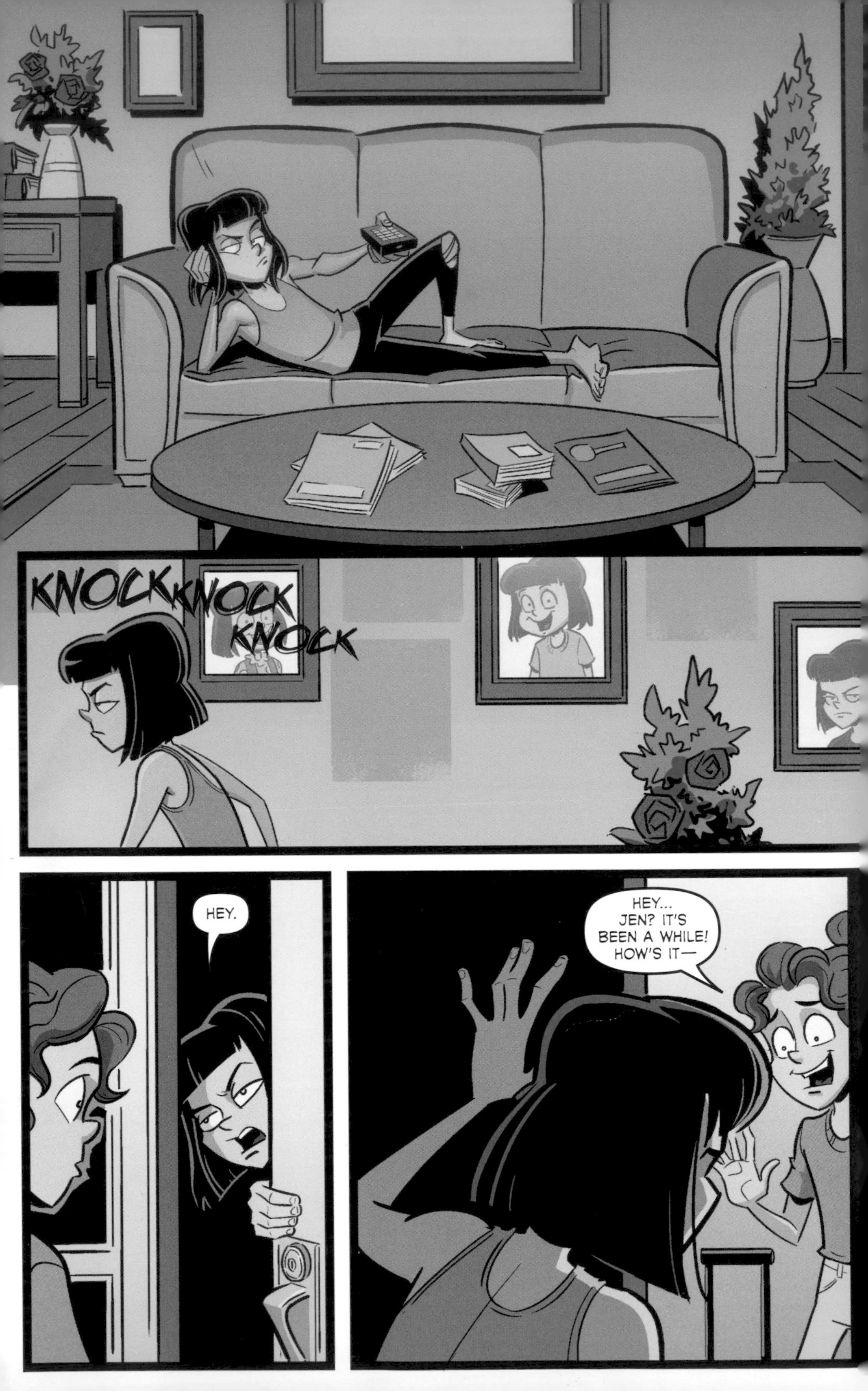
KNOCK KNOCK KNOCK
HEY.
HEY... JEN? IT'S BEEN A WHILE! HOW'S IT—

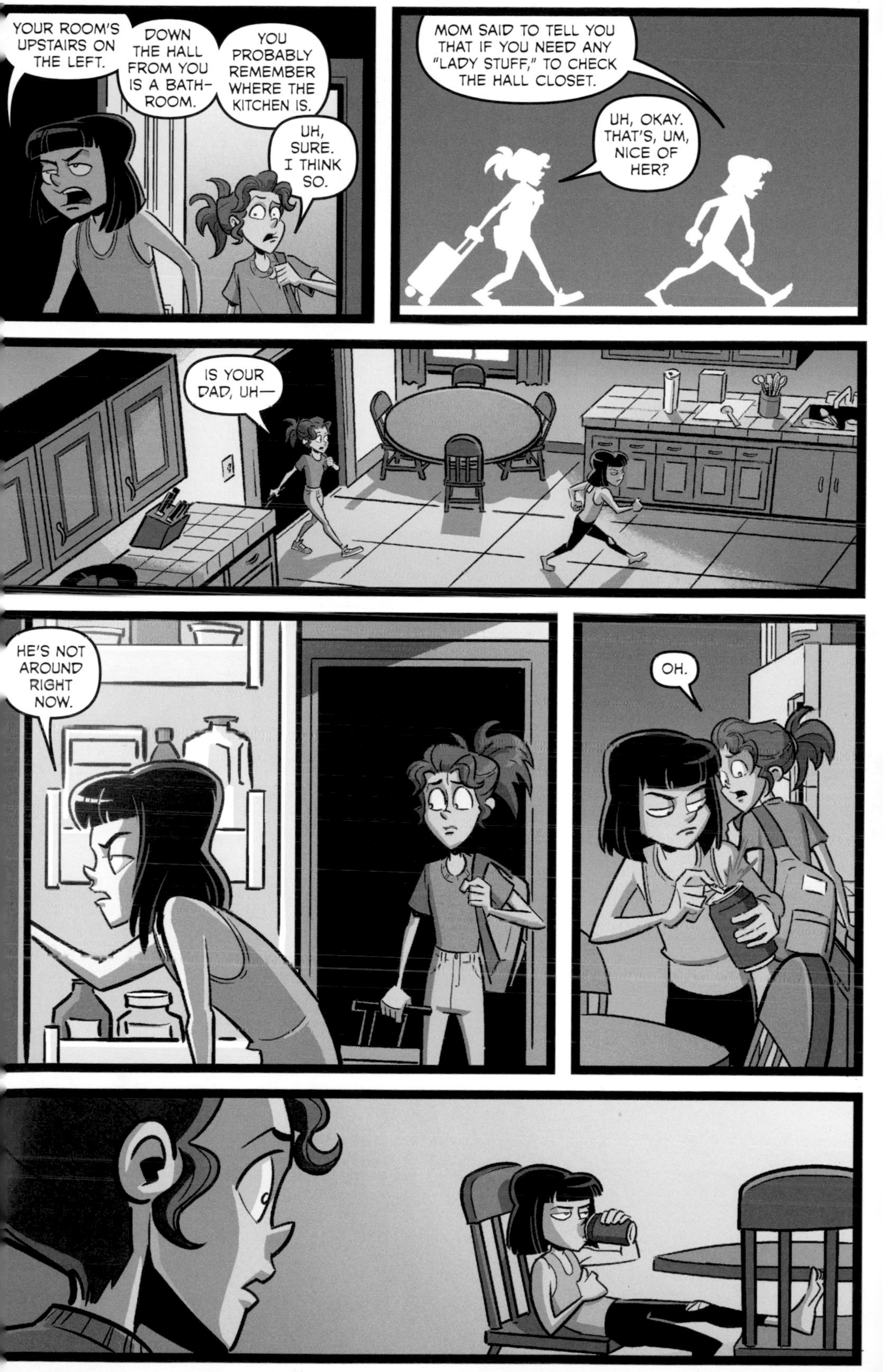
YOUR ROOM'S UPSTAIRS ON THE LEFT.
DOWN THE HALL FROM YOU IS A BATH-ROOM.
YOU PROBABLY REMEMBER WHERE THE KITCHEN IS.
UH, SURE. I THINK SO.
MOM SAID TO TELL YOU THAT IF YOU NEED ANY "LADY STUFF," TO CHECK THE HALL CLOSET.
UH, OKAY. THAT'S, UM, NICE OF HER?
IS YOUR DAD, UH—
HE'S NOT AROUND RIGHT NOW.
OH.

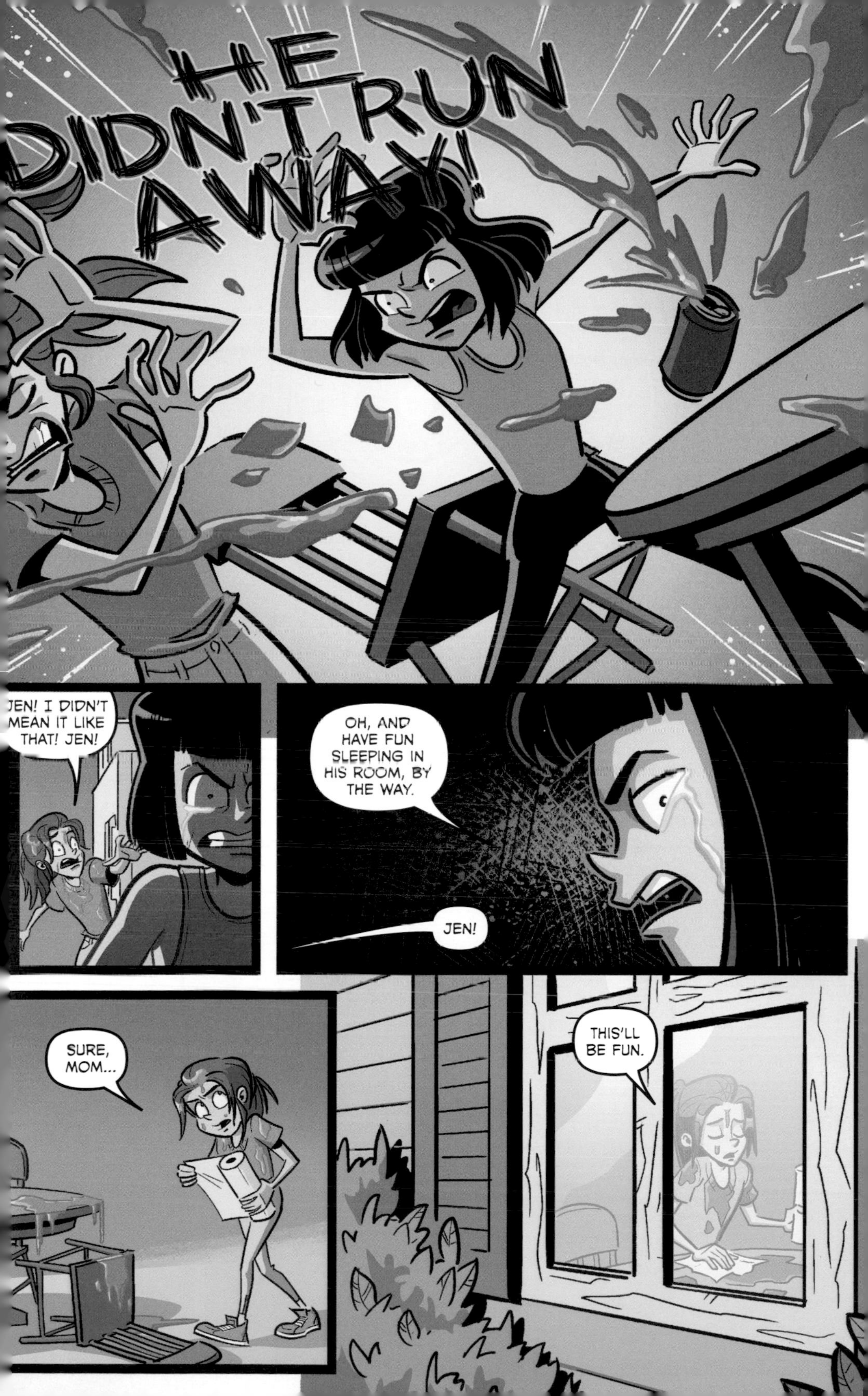
HE DIDN'T RUN AWAY!
JEN! I DIDN'T MEAN IT LIKE THAT! JEN!
OH, AND HAVE FUN SLEEPING IN HIS ROOM, BY THE WAY.
JEN!
SURE, MOM...
THIS'LL BE FUN.

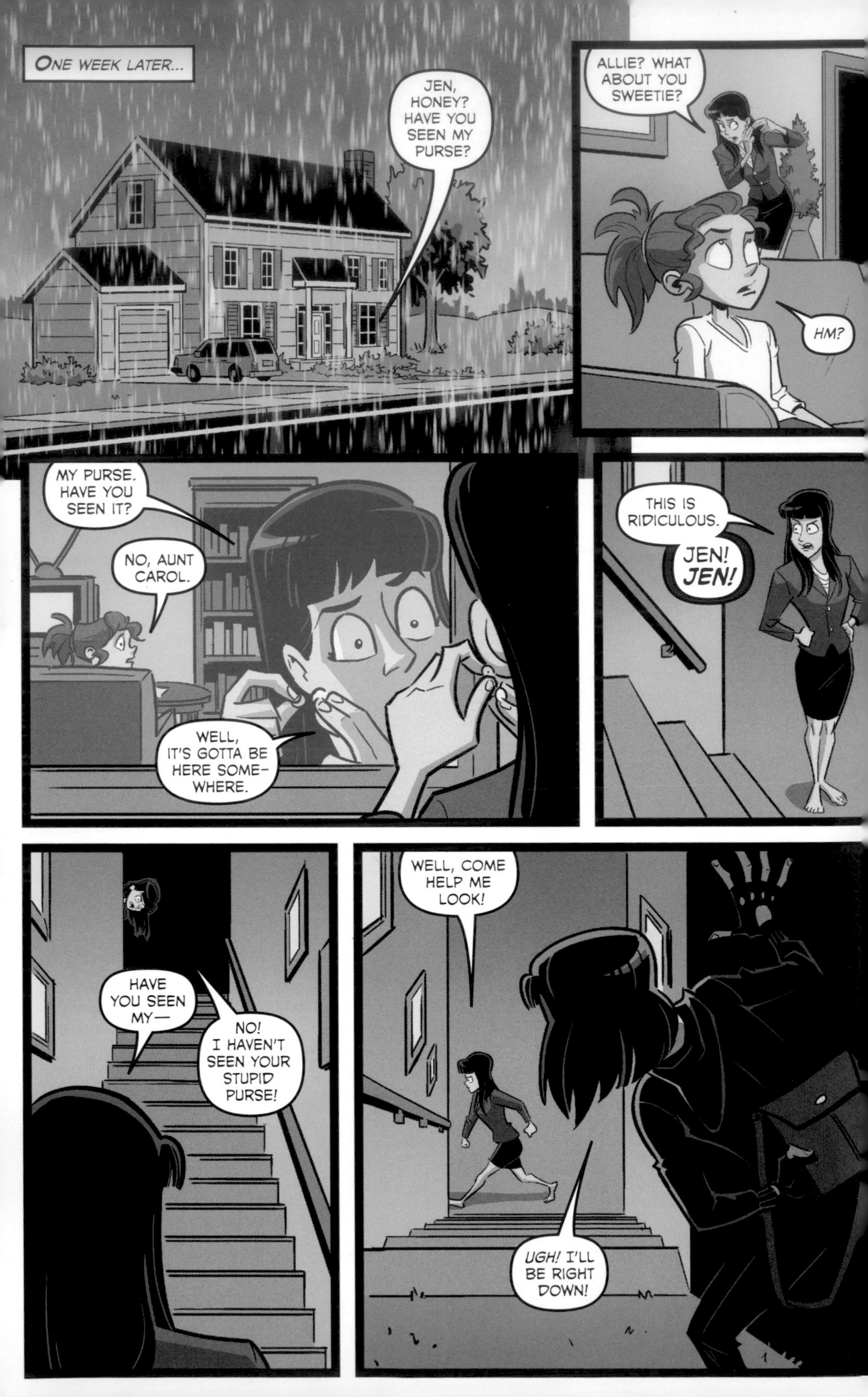
ONE WEEK LATER...
JEN, HONEY? HAVE YOU SEEN MY PURSE?
ALLIE? WHAT ABOUT YOU SWEETIE?
HM?
MY PURSE. HAVE YOU SEEN IT?
NO, AUNT CAROL.
WELL, IT'S GOTTA BE HERE SOME-WHERE.
THIS IS RIDICULOUS.
JEN! JEN!
HAVE YOU SEEN MY—
NO! I HAVEN'T SEEN YOUR STUPID PURSE!
WELL, COME HELP ME LOOK!
UGH! I'LL BE RIGHT DOWN!

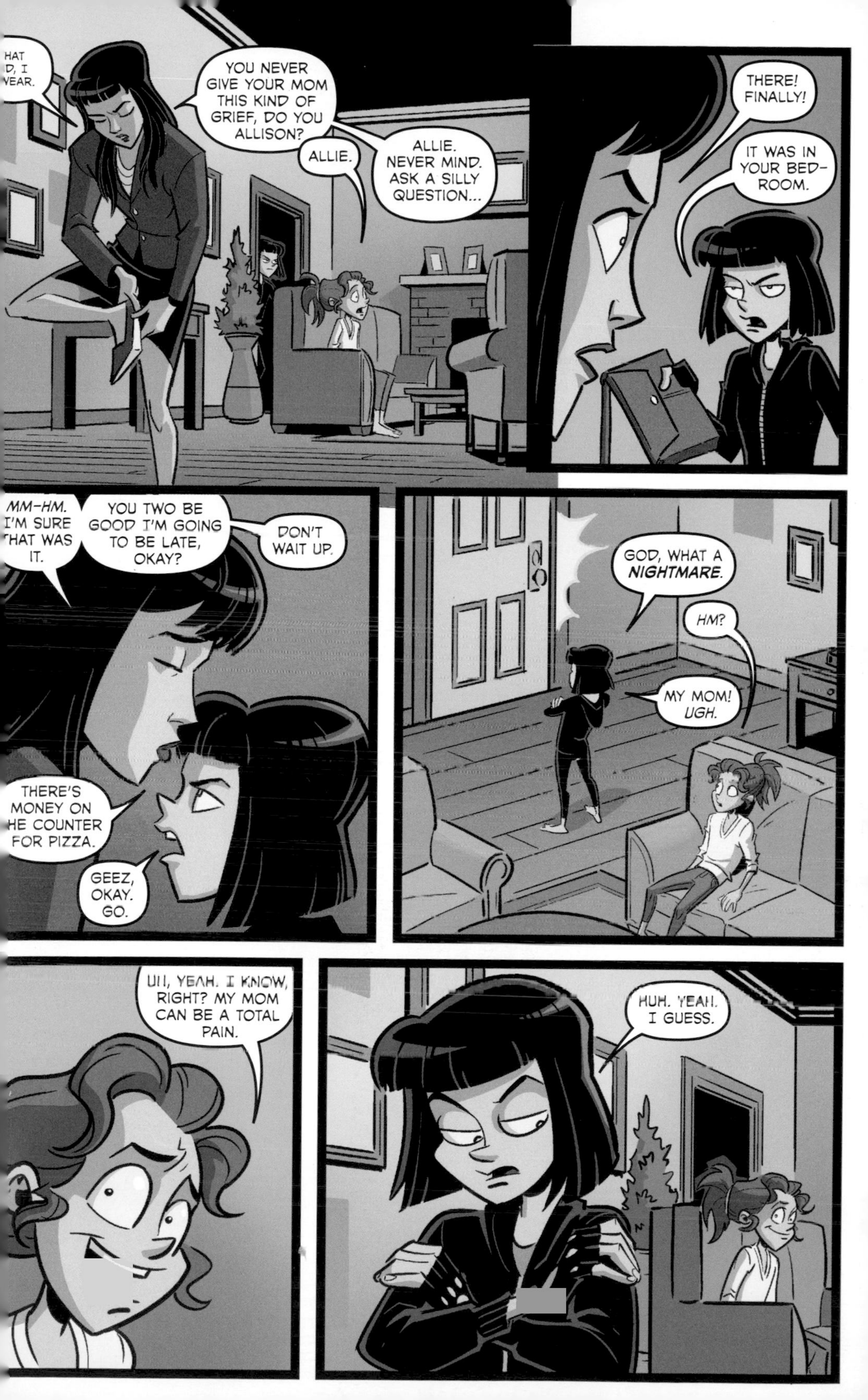
HAT D, I VEAR.
YOU NEVER GIVE YOUR MOM THIS KIND OF GRIEF, DO YOU ALLISON?
ALLIE.
ALLIE. NEVER MIND. ASK A SILLY QUESTION...
THERE! FINALLY!
IT WAS IN YOUR BED-ROOM.
MM-HM. I'M SURE THAT WAS IT.
YOU TWO BE GOOD I'M GOING TO BE LATE, OKAY?
DON'T WAIT UP.
THERE'S MONEY ON HE COUNTER FOR PIZZA.
GEEZ, OKAY. GO.
GOD, WHAT A NIGHTMARE.
HM?
MY MOM! UGH.
UH, YEAH. I KNOW, RIGHT? MY MOM CAN BE A TOTAL PAIN.
HUH. YEAH. I GUESS.

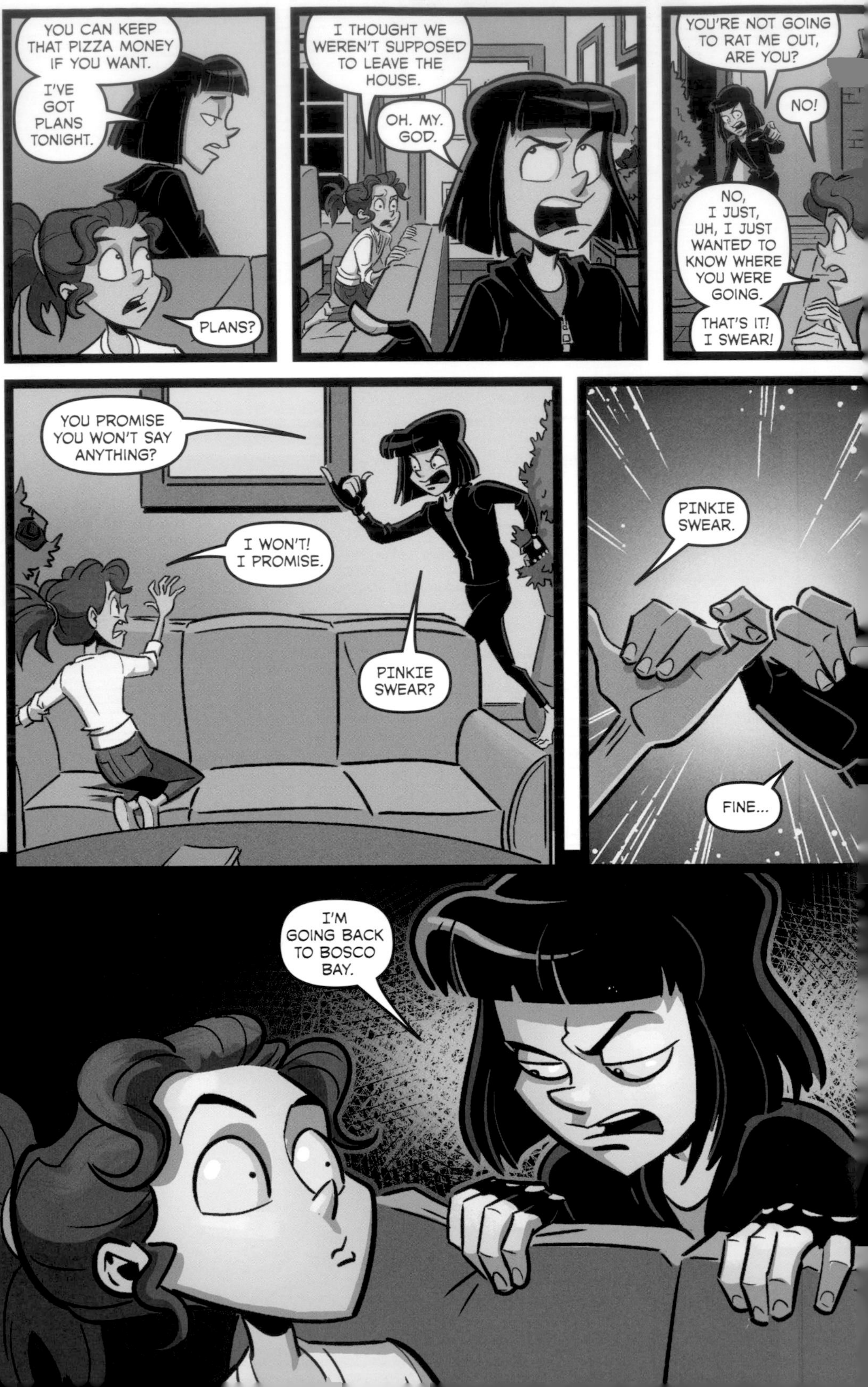
YOU CAN KEEP THAT PIZZA MONEY IF YOU WANT.
I'VE GOT PLANS TONIGHT.
PLANS?
I THOUGHT WE WEREN'T SUPPOSED TO LEAVE THE HOUSE.
OH. MY. GOD.
YOU'RE NOT GOING TO RAT ME OUT, ARE YOU?
NO!
NO, I JUST, UH, I JUST WANTED TO KNOW WHERE YOU WERE GOING.
THAT'S IT! I SWEAR!
YOU PROMISE YOU WON'T SAY ANYTHING?
I WON'T! I PROMISE.
PINKIE SWEAR?
PINKIE SWEAR.
FINE...
I'M GOING BACK TO BOSCO BAY.

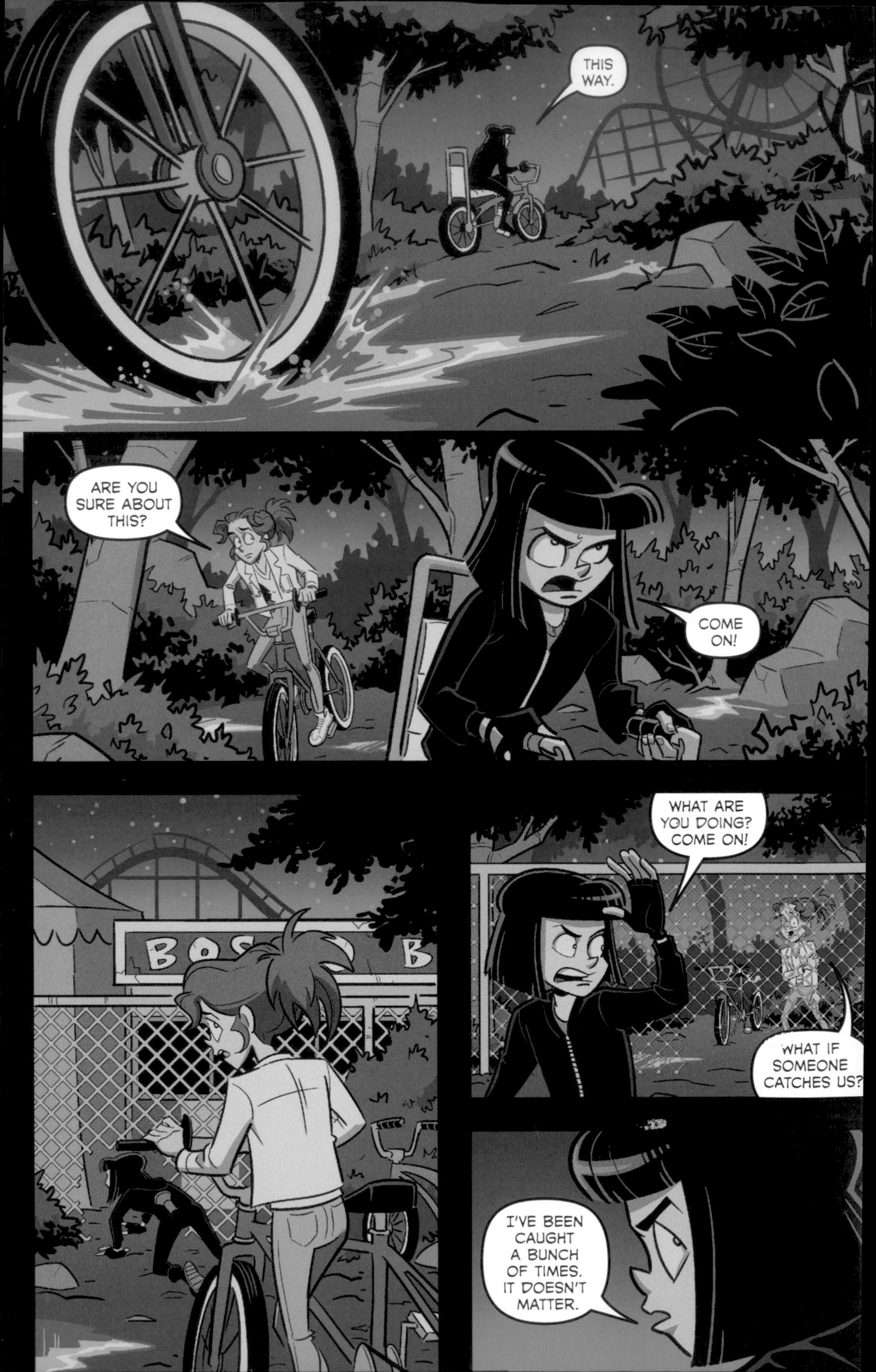
THIS WAY.
ARE YOU SURE ABOUT THIS?
COME ON!
BOS B
WHAT ARE YOU DOING? COME ON!
WHAT IF SOMEONE CATCHES US?
I'VE BEEN CAUGHT A BUNCH OF TIMES. IT DOESN'T MATTER.

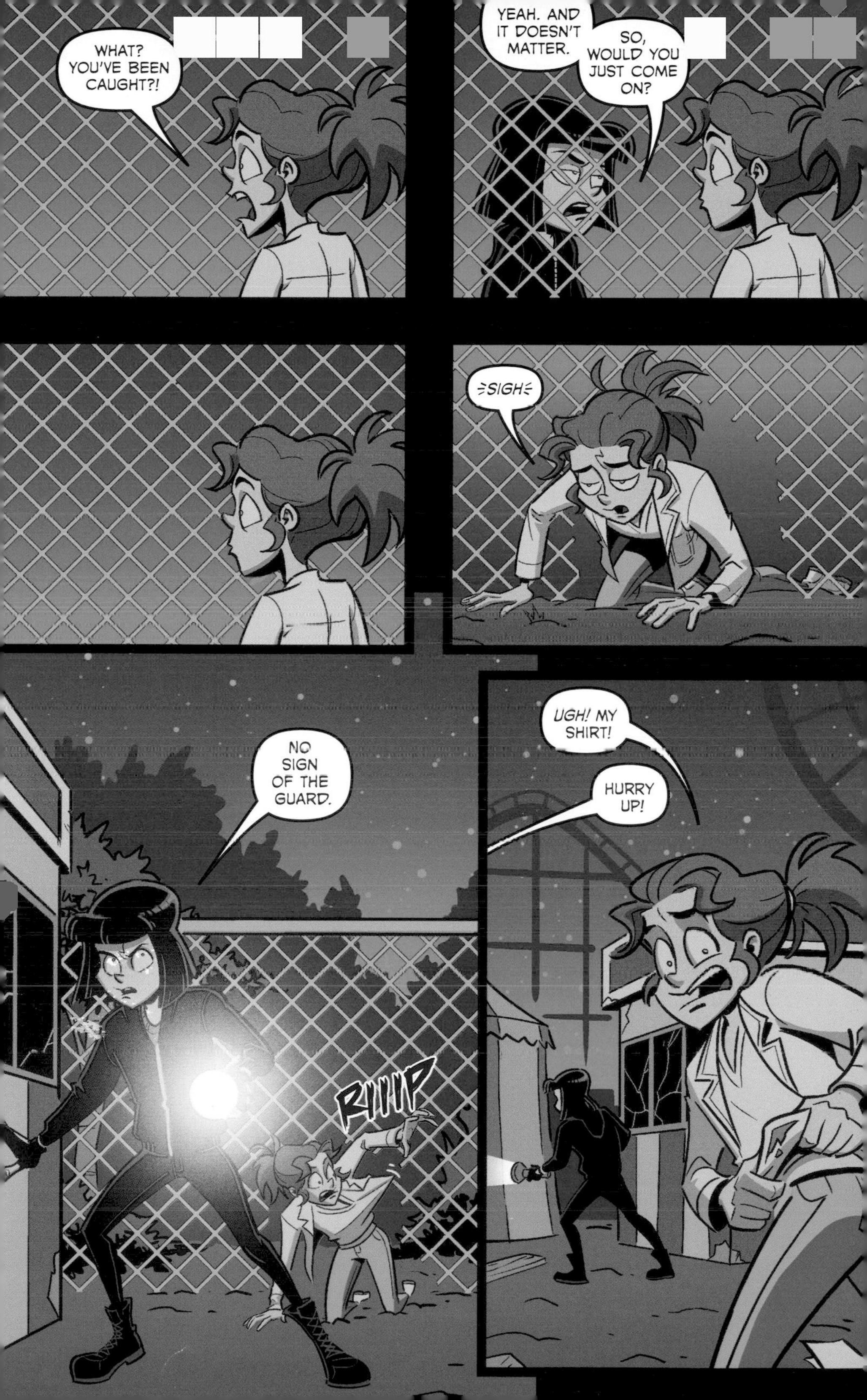
WHAT? YOU'VE BEEN CAUGHT?!
YEAH. AND IT DOESN'T MATTER.
SO, WOULD YOU JUST COME ON?
SIGH
NO SIGN OF THE GUARD.
RIIIP
UGH! MY SHIRT!
HURRY UP!

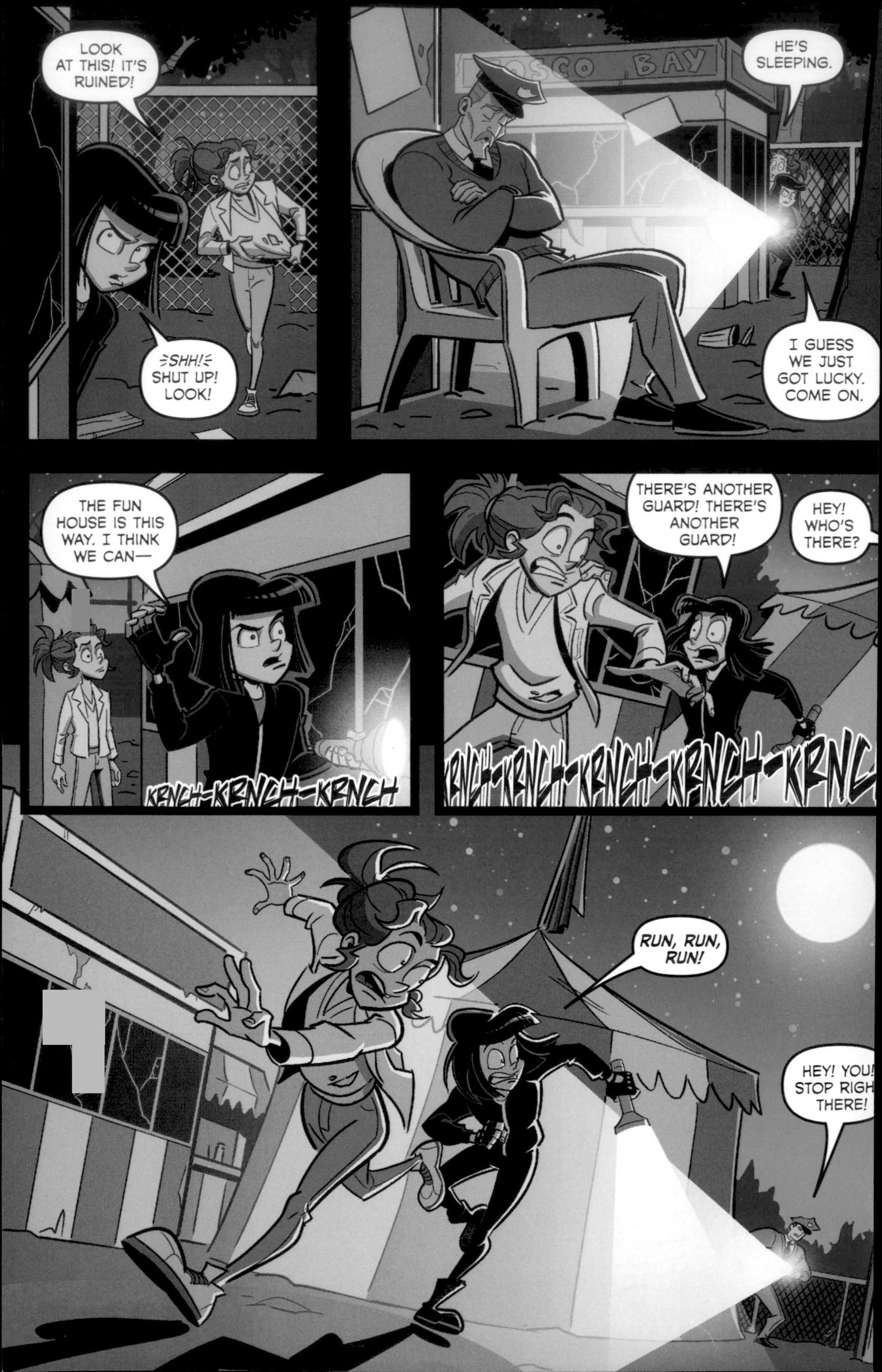
LOOK AT THIS! IT'S RUINED!
SHH! SHUT UP! LOOK!
HE'S SLEEPING.
I GUESS WE JUST GOT LUCKY. COME ON.
THE FUN HOUSE IS THIS WAY. I THINK WE CAN—
KRNCH-KRNCH-KRNCH
THERE'S ANOTHER GUARD! THERE'S ANOTHER GUARD!
HEY! WHO'S THERE?
KRNCH-KRNCH-KRNCH-KRNCH-KRNC
RUN, RUN, RUN!
HEY! YOU! STOP RIGH THERE!

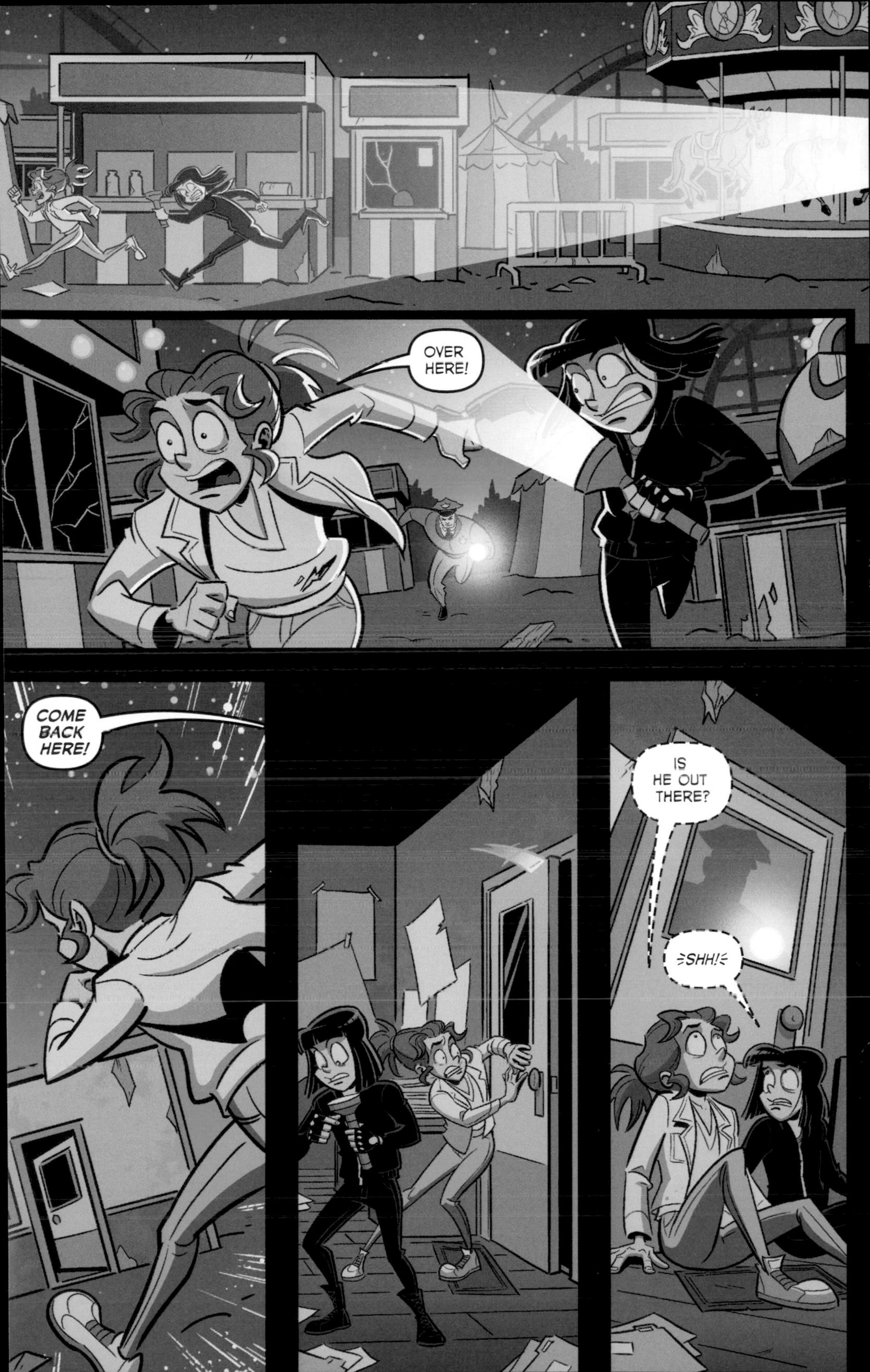
OVER HERE!
COME BACK HERE!
IS HE OUT THERE?
SHH!

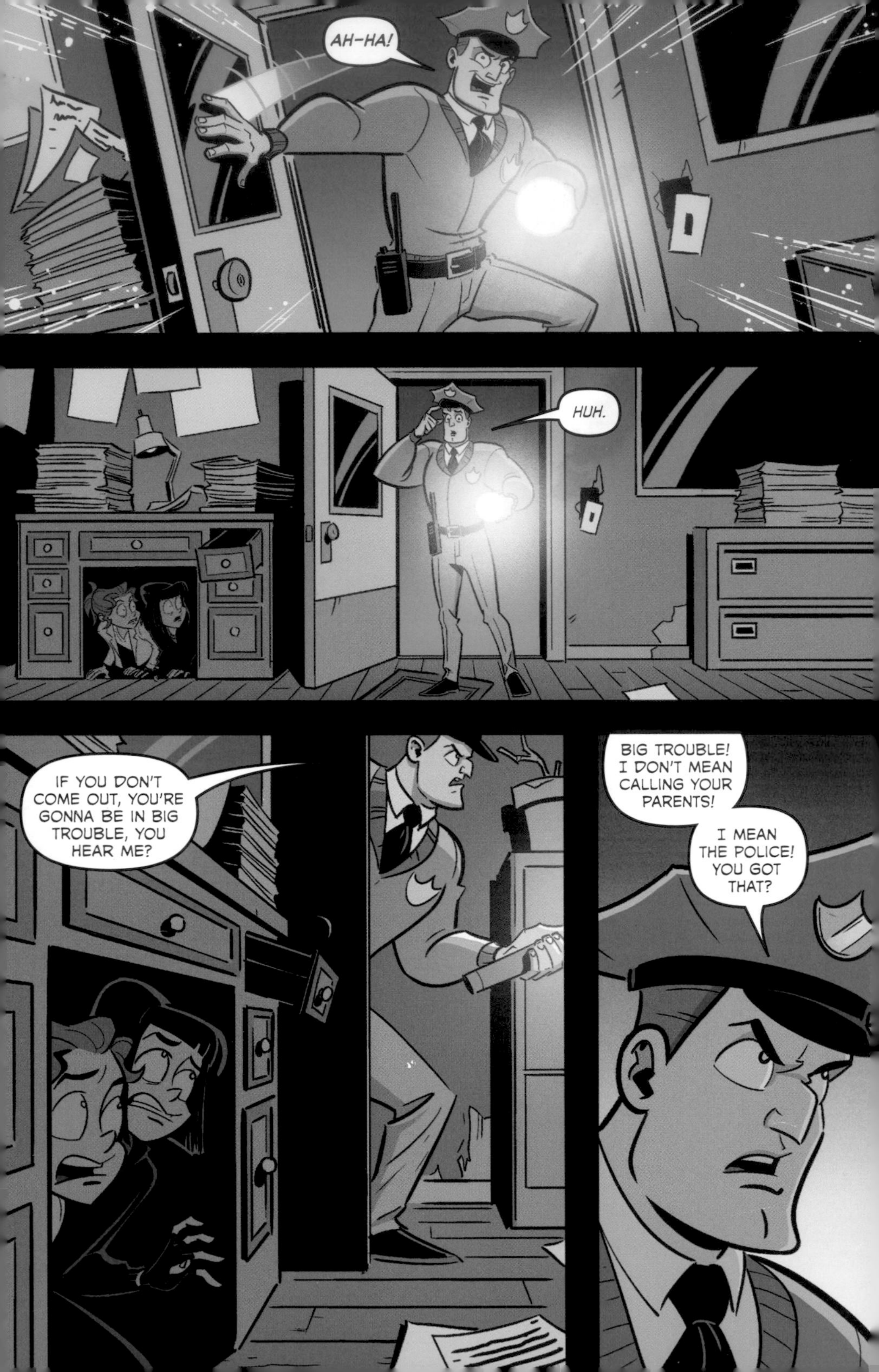
AH-HA!
HUH.
IF YOU DON'T COME OUT, YOU'RE GONNA BE IN BIG TROUBLE, YOU HEAR ME?
BIG TROUBLE! I DON'T MEAN CALLING YOUR PARENTS!
I MEAN THE POLICE! YOU GOT THAT?

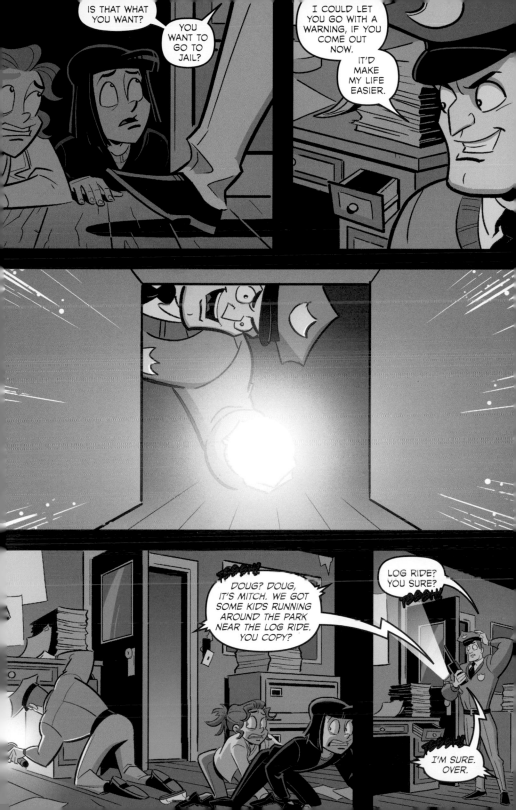

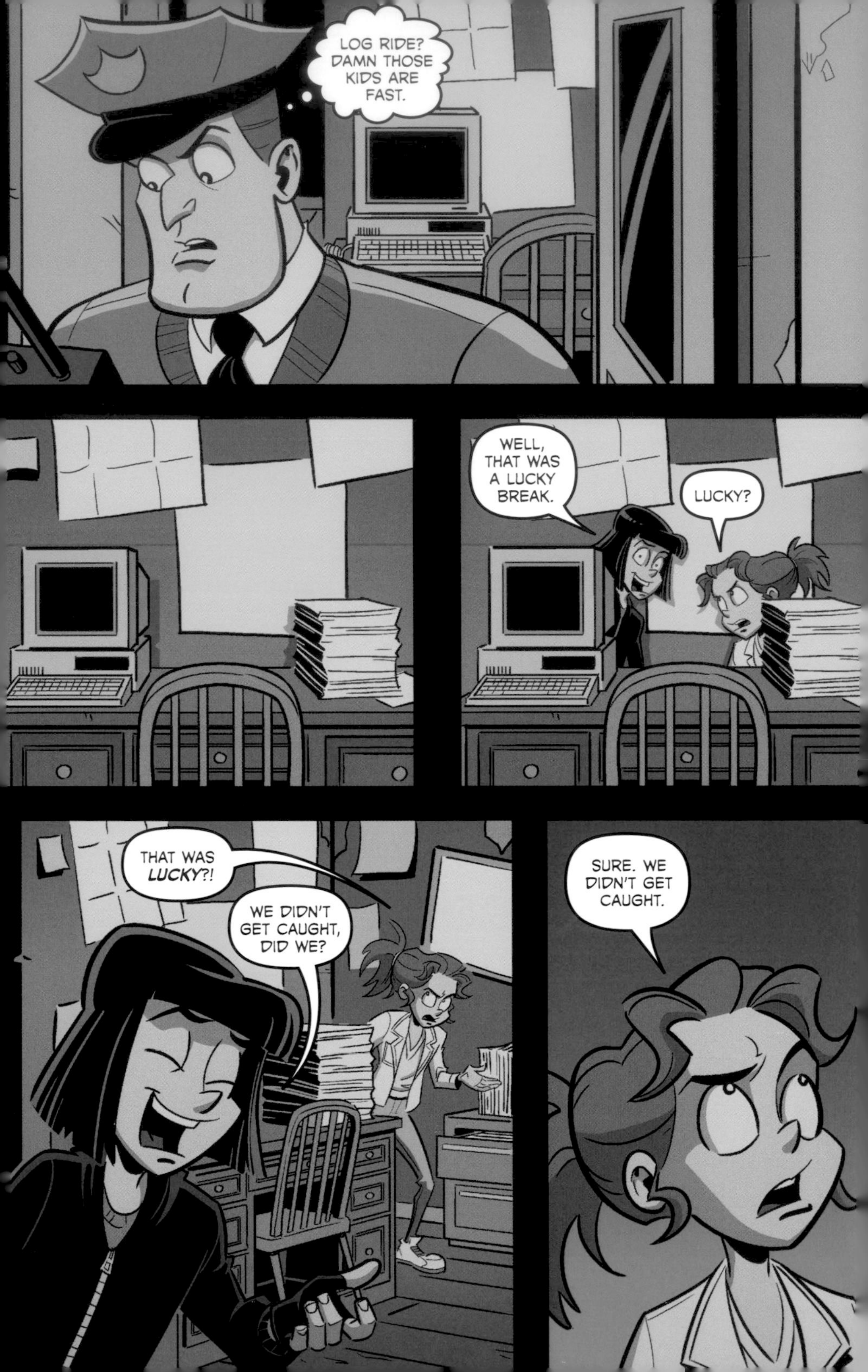
LOG RIDE? DAMN THOSE KIDS ARE FAST.
WELL, THAT WAS A LUCKY BREAK.
LUCKY?
THAT WAS *LUCKY*?!
WE DIDN'T GET CAUGHT, DID WE?
SURE. WE DIDN'T GET CAUGHT.

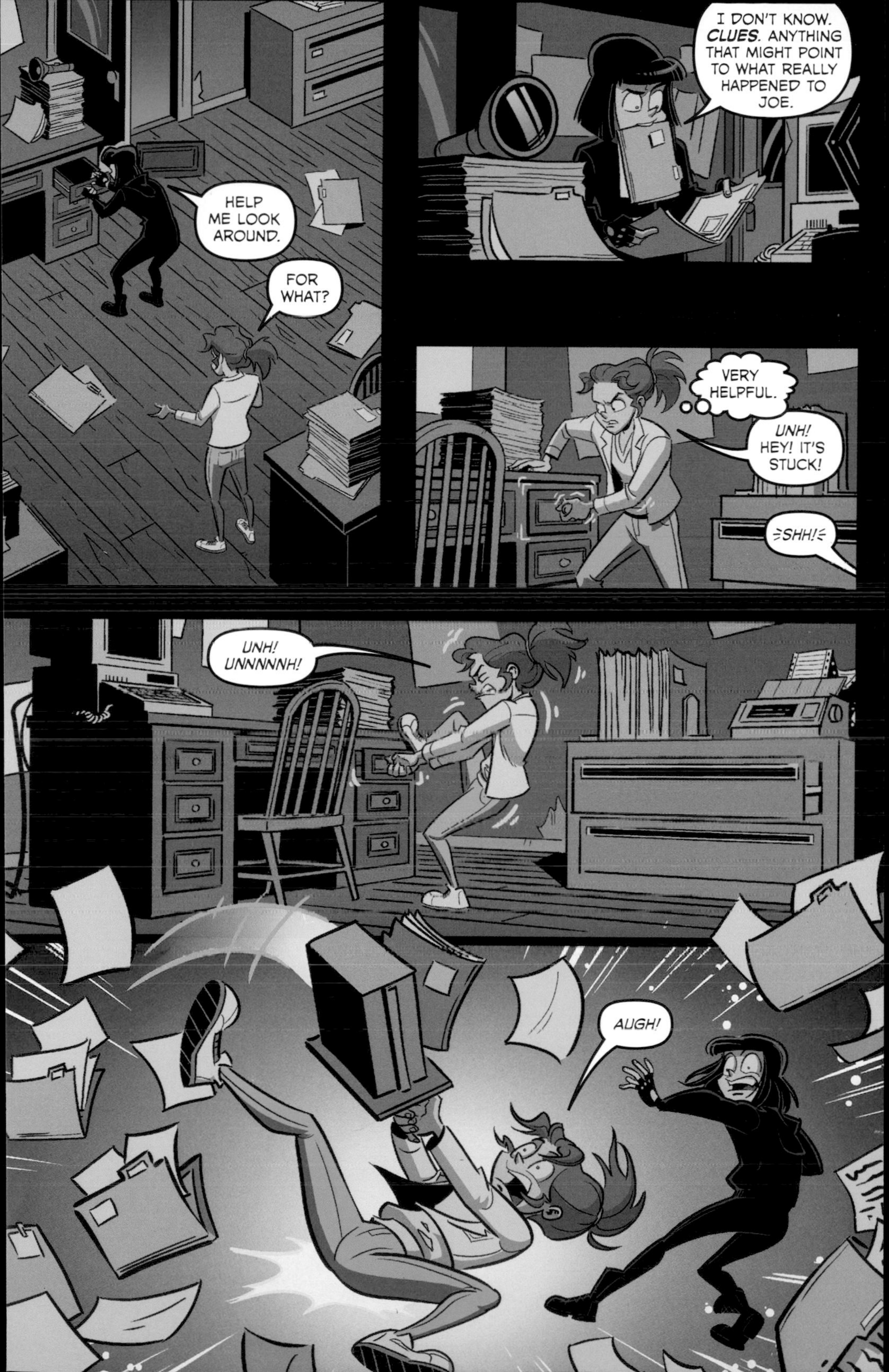
HELP ME LOOK AROUND.
FOR WHAT?
I DON'T KNOW. **CLUES.** ANYTHING THAT MIGHT POINT TO WHAT REALLY HAPPENED TO JOE.
VERY HELPFUL.
UNH! HEY! IT'S STUCK!
SHH!
UNH! UNNNNNH!
AUGH!

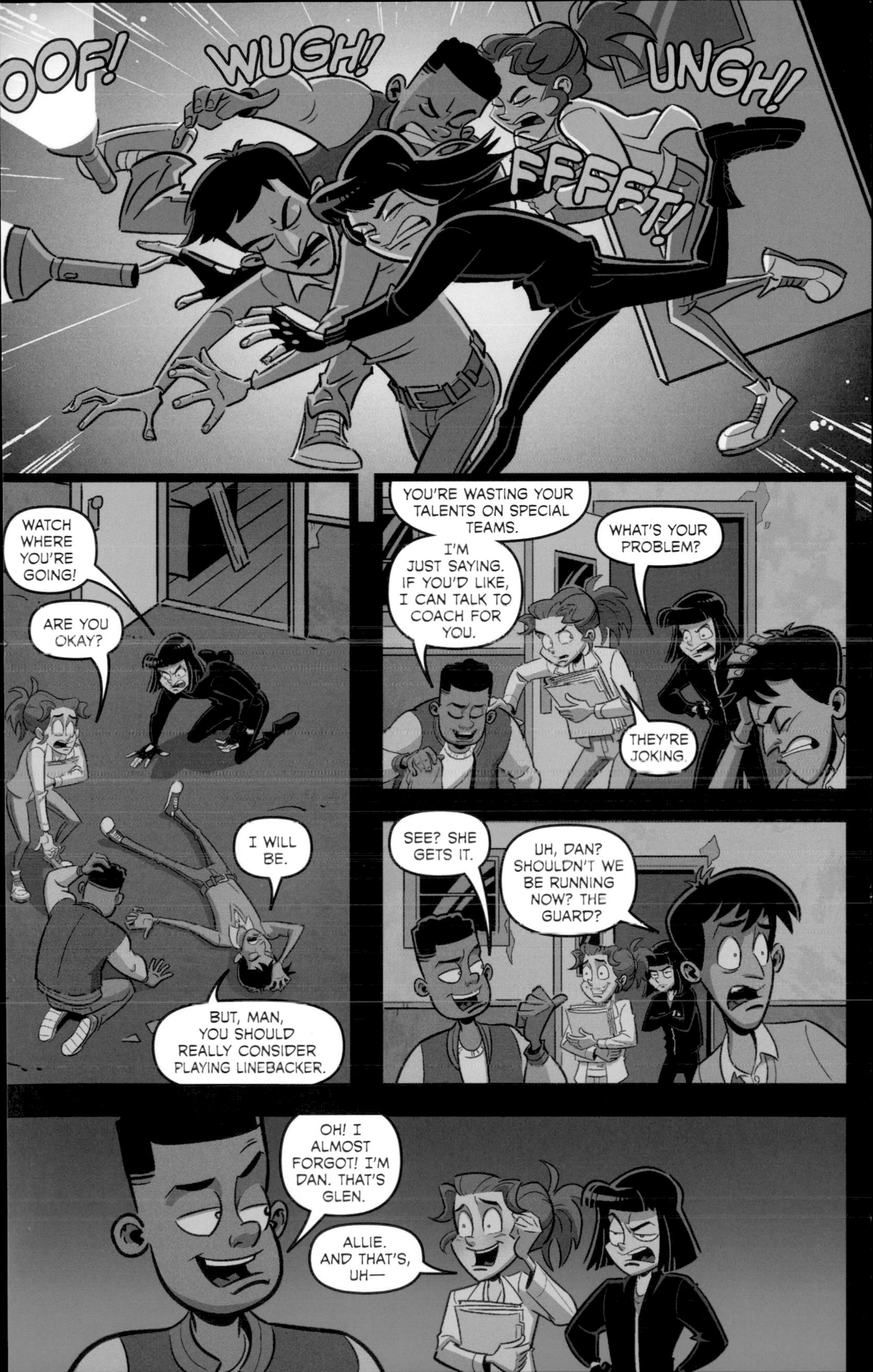
OOF!
WUGH!
UNGH!
FFFFT!
WATCH WHERE YOU'RE GOING!
ARE YOU OKAY?
I WILL BE.
BUT, MAN, YOU SHOULD REALLY CONSIDER PLAYING LINEBACKER.
YOU'RE WASTING YOUR TALENTS ON SPECIAL TEAMS.
I'M JUST SAYING. IF YOU'D LIKE, I CAN TALK TO COACH FOR YOU.
WHAT'S YOUR PROBLEM?
THEY'RE JOKING.
SEE? SHE GETS IT.
UH, DAN? SHOULDN'T WE BE RUNNING NOW? THE GUARD?
OH! I ALMOST FORGOT! I'M DAN. THAT'S GLEN.
ALLIE. AND THAT'S, UH—

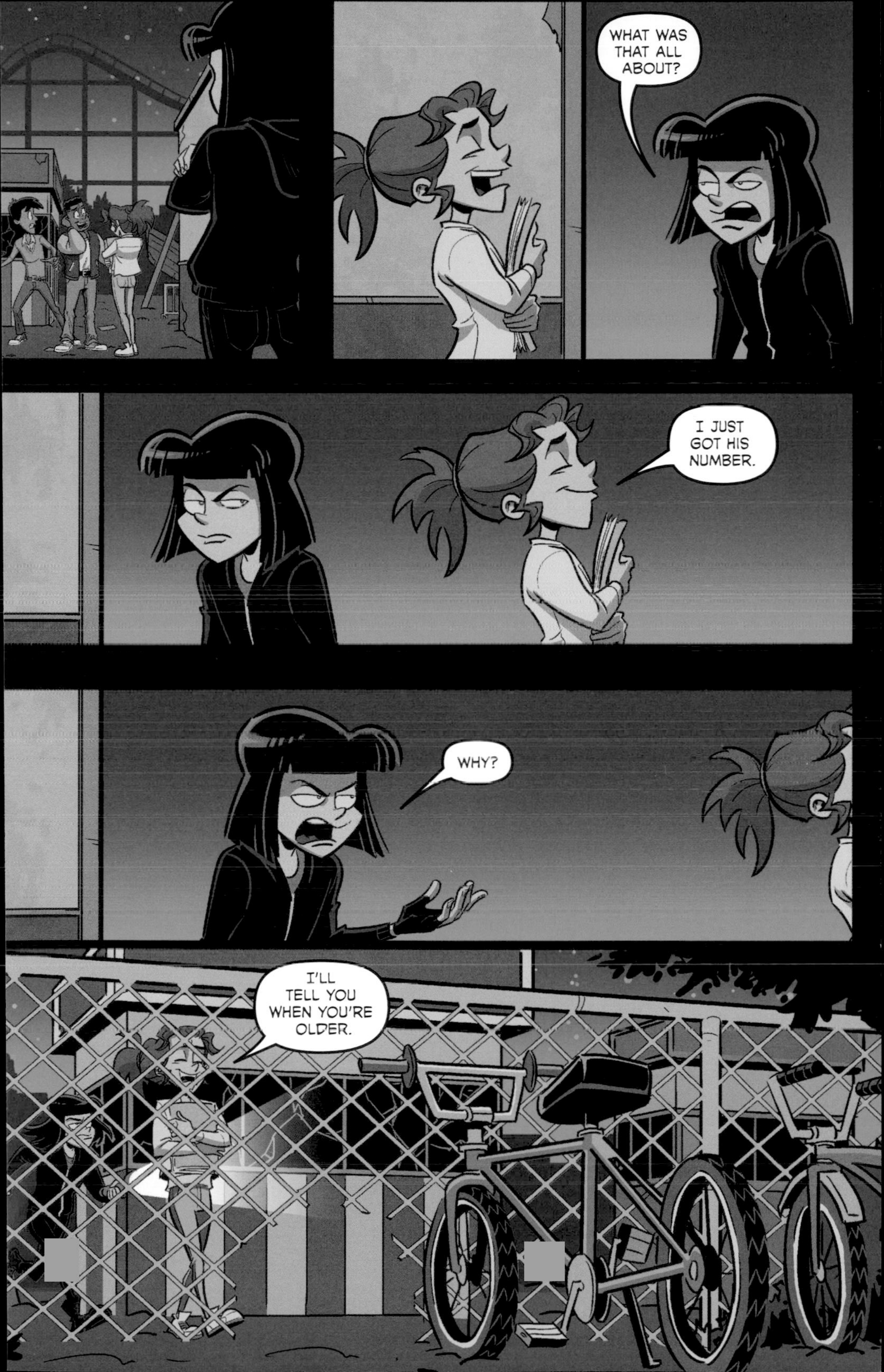
WHAT WAS THAT ALL ABOUT?
I JUST GOT HIS NUMBER.
WHY?
I'LL TELL YOU WHEN YOU'RE OLDER.

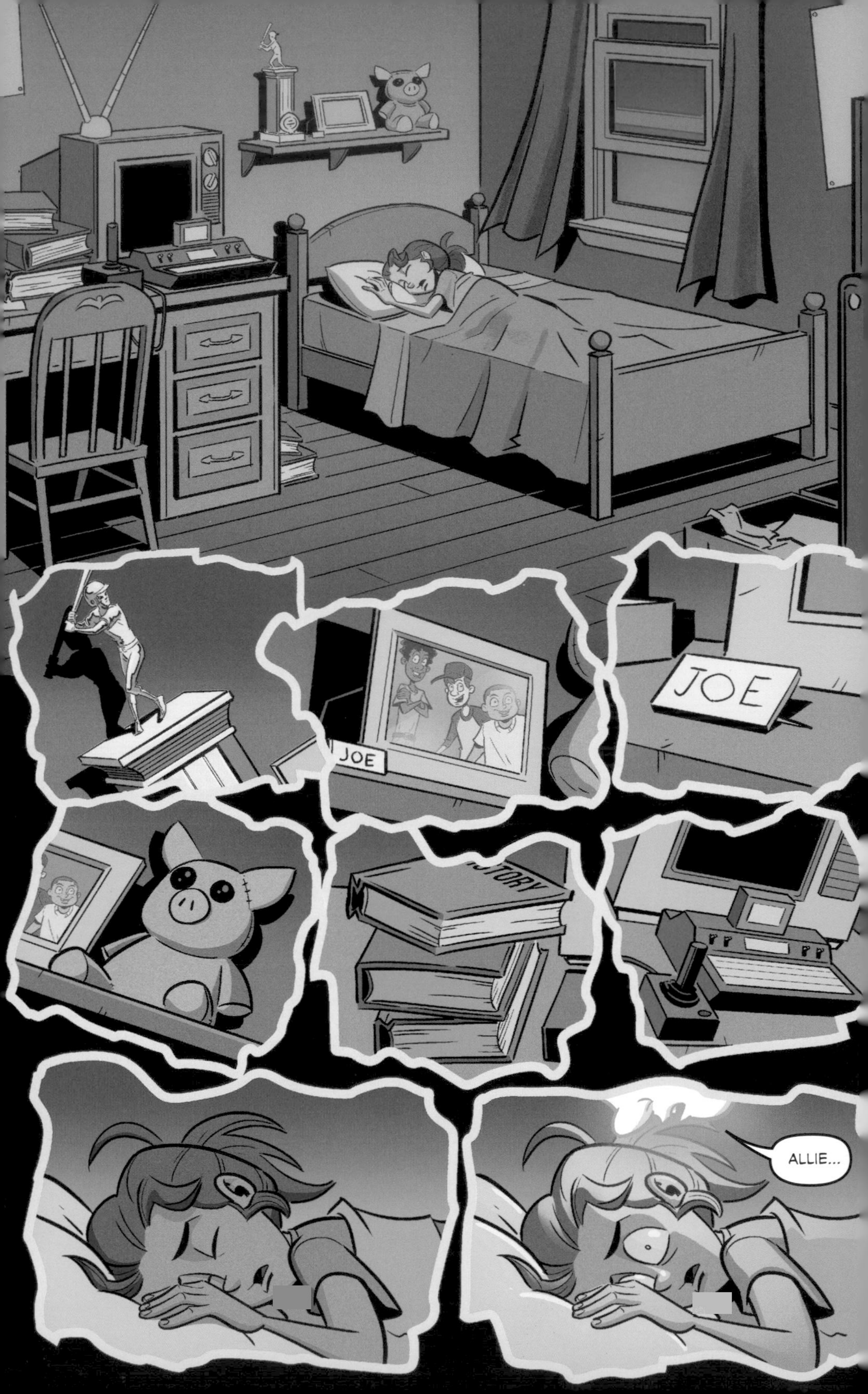
JOE
JOE
ALLIE...

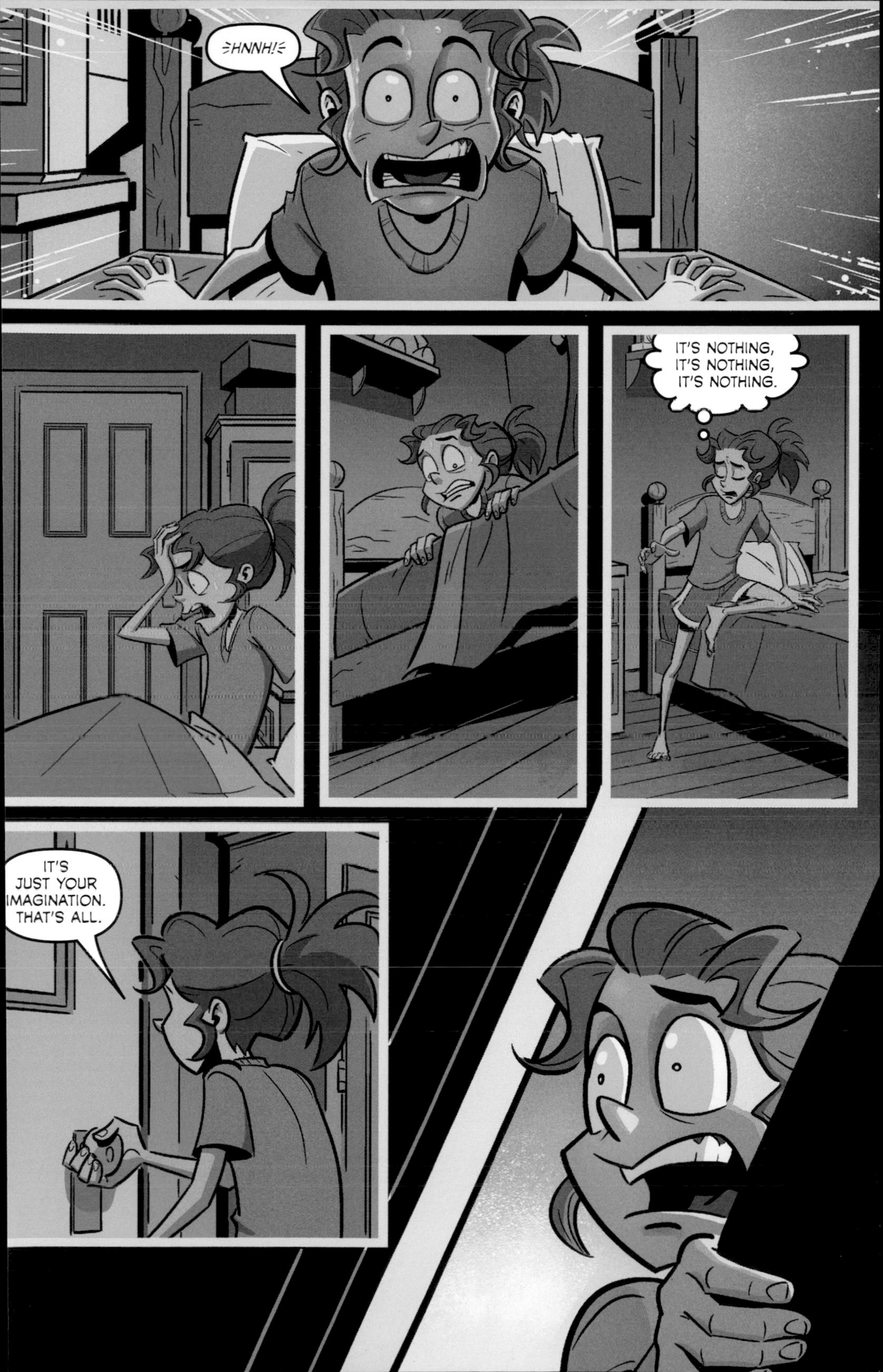
HNNH!
IT'S NOTHING, IT'S NOTHING, IT'S NOTHING.
IT'S JUST YOUR IMAGINATION. THAT'S ALL.

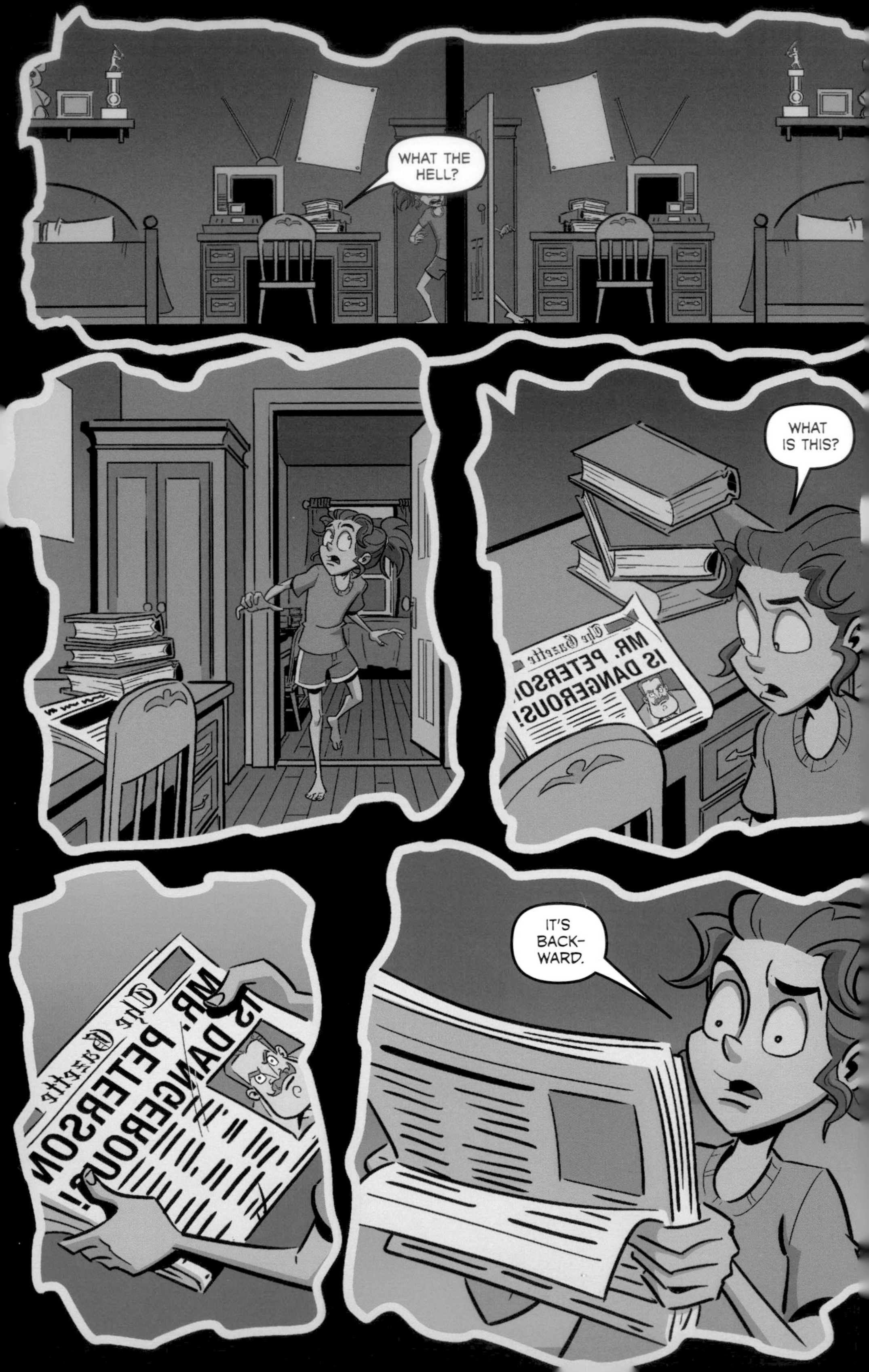
WHAT THE HELL?
WHAT IS THIS?
The Gazette
MR. PETERSON IS DANGEROUS!
IT'S BACK-WARD.

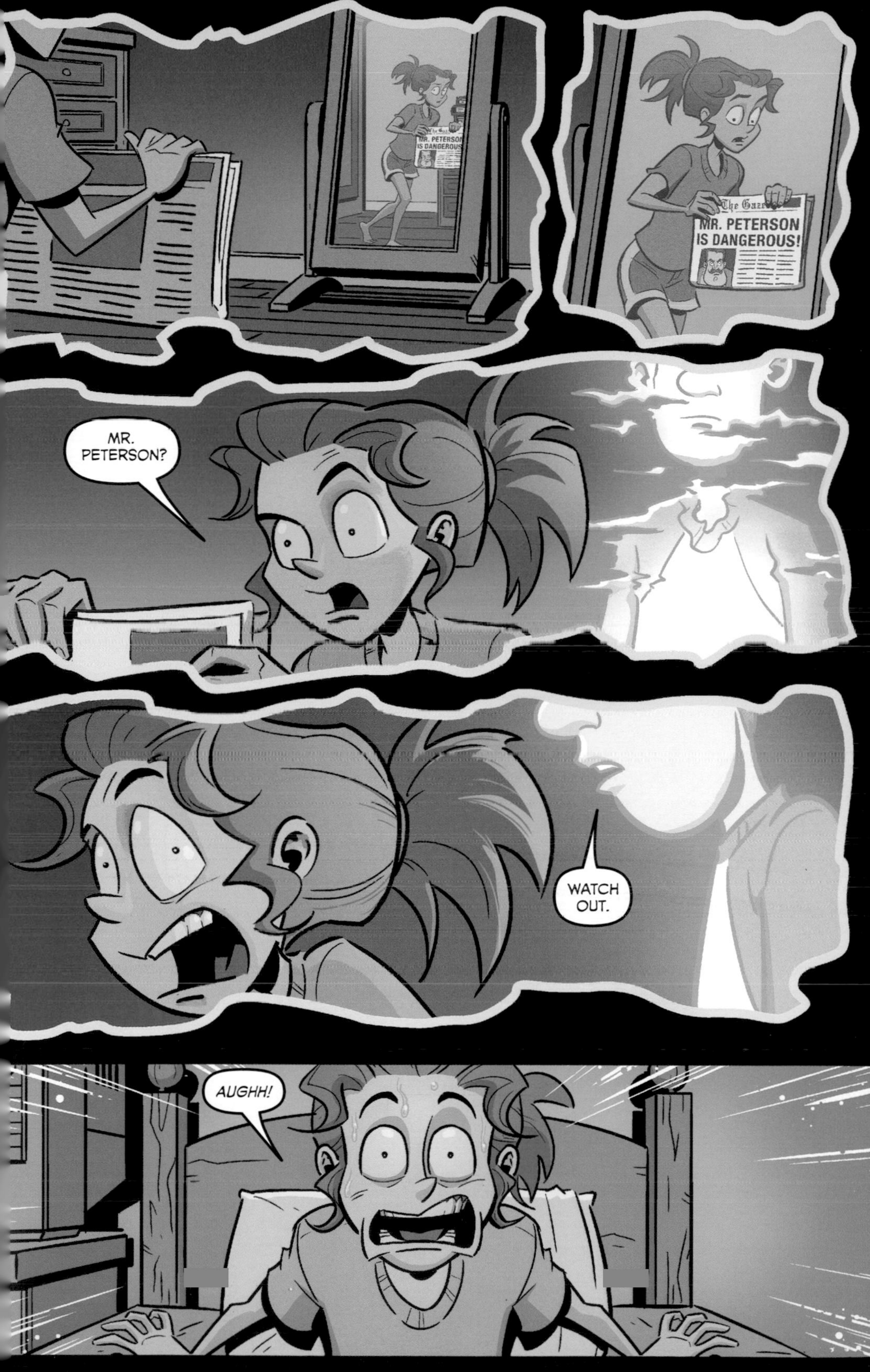
MR. PETERSON IS DANGEROUS
The Gazette
MR. PETERSON IS DANGEROUS!
MR. PETERSON?
WATCH OUT.
AUGHH!

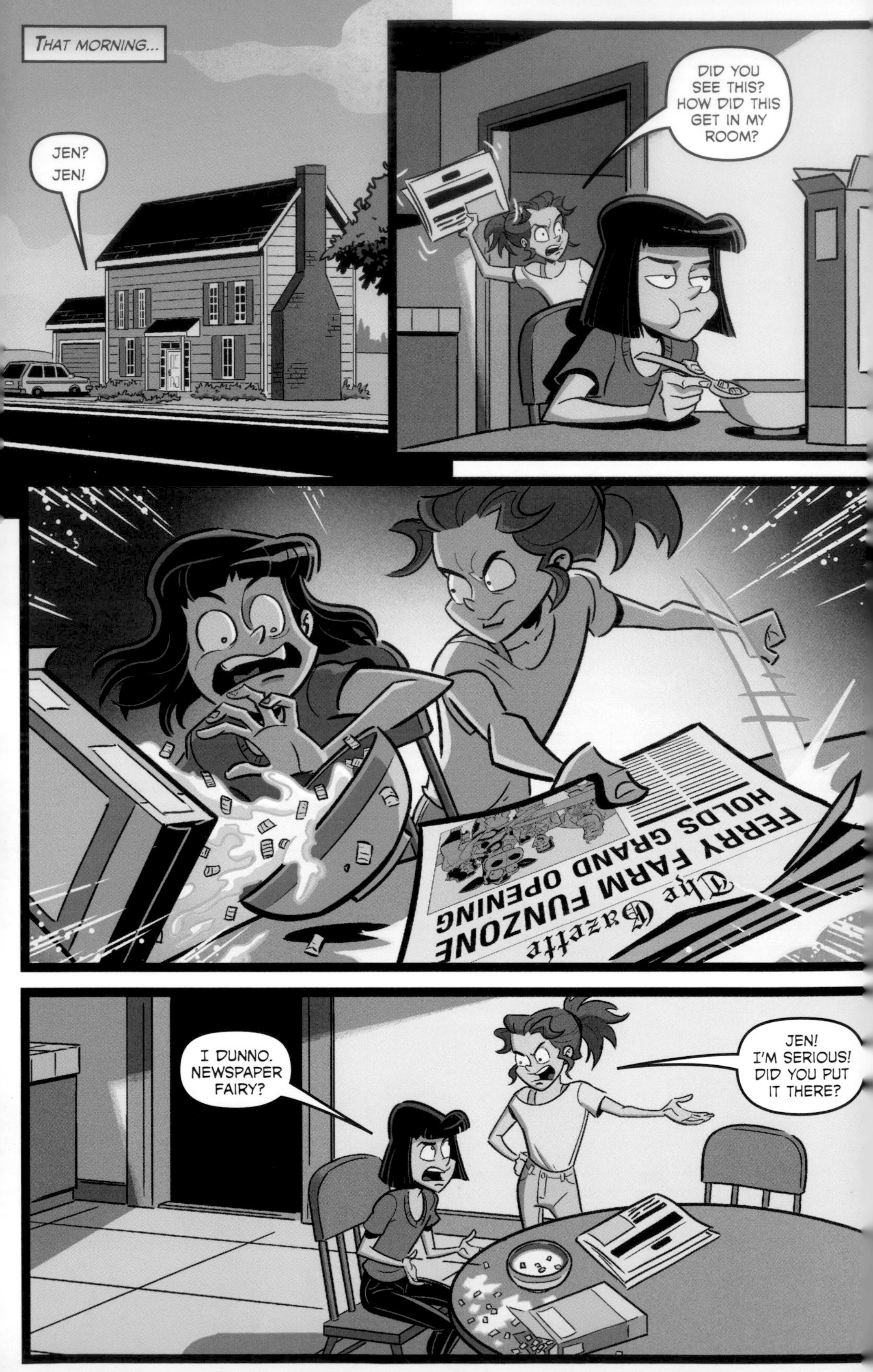

THAT MORNING...
JEN? JEN!
DID YOU SEE THIS? HOW DID THIS GET IN MY ROOM?
The Gazette
FERRY FARM FUNZONE HOLDS GRAND OPENING
I DUNNO. NEWSPAPER FAIRY?
JEN! I'M SERIOUS! DID YOU PUT IT THERE?

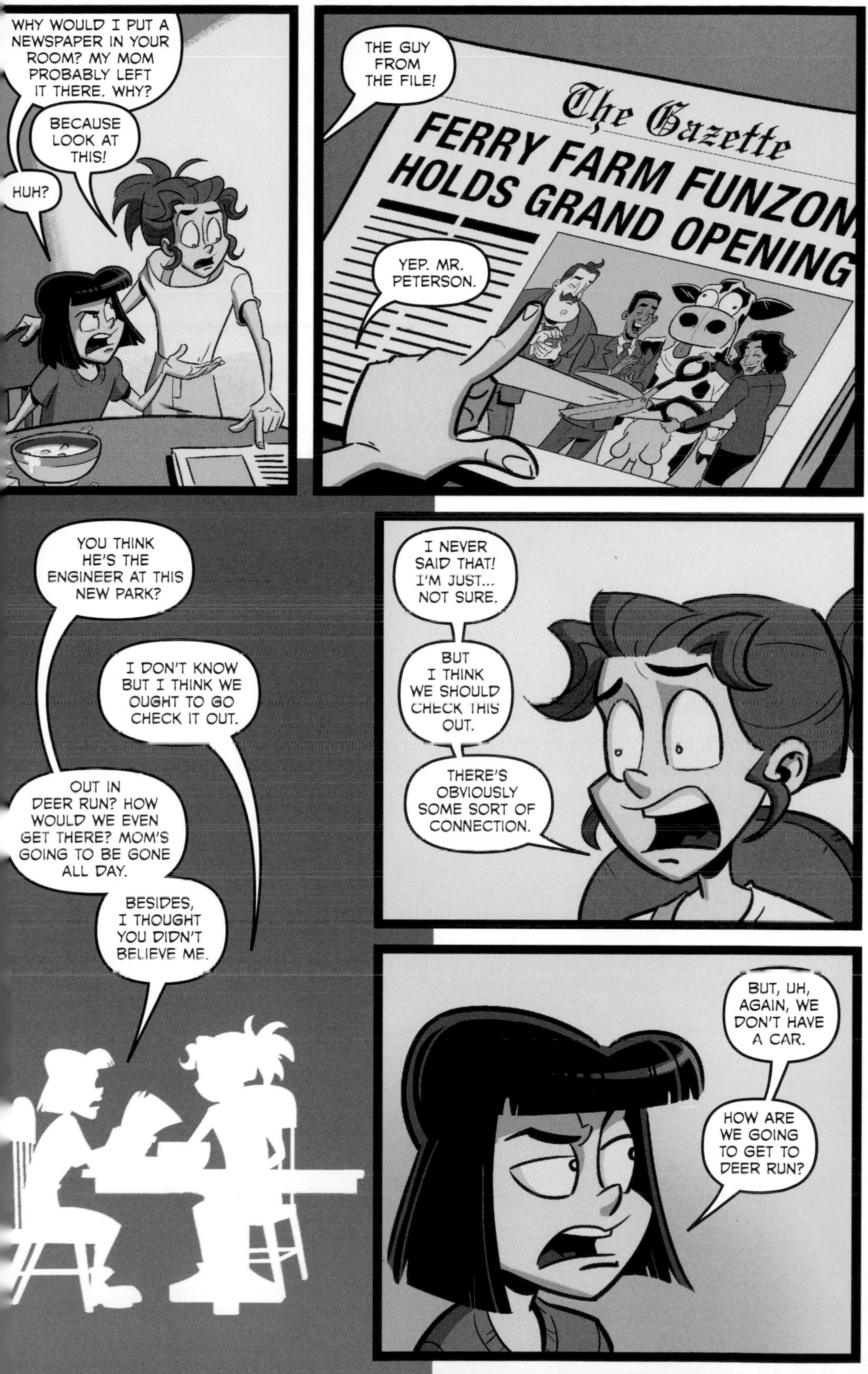
WHY WOULD I PUT A NEWSPAPER IN YOUR ROOM? MY MOM PROBABLY LEFT IT THERE. WHY?
BECAUSE LOOK AT THIS!
HUH?
THE GUY FROM THE FILE!
The Gazette
FERRY FARM FUNZONE HOLDS GRAND OPENING
YEP. MR. PETERSON.
YOU THINK HE'S THE ENGINEER AT THIS NEW PARK?
I DON'T KNOW BUT I THINK WE OUGHT TO GO CHECK IT OUT.
OUT IN DEER RUN? HOW WOULD WE EVEN GET THERE? MOM'S GOING TO BE GONE ALL DAY.
BESIDES, I THOUGHT YOU DIDN'T BELIEVE ME.
I NEVER SAID THAT! I'M JUST... NOT SURE.
BUT I THINK WE SHOULD CHECK THIS OUT.
THERE'S OBVIOUSLY SOME SORT OF CONNECTION.
BUT, UH, AGAIN, WE DON'T HAVE A CAR.
HOW ARE WE GOING TO GET TO DEER RUN?

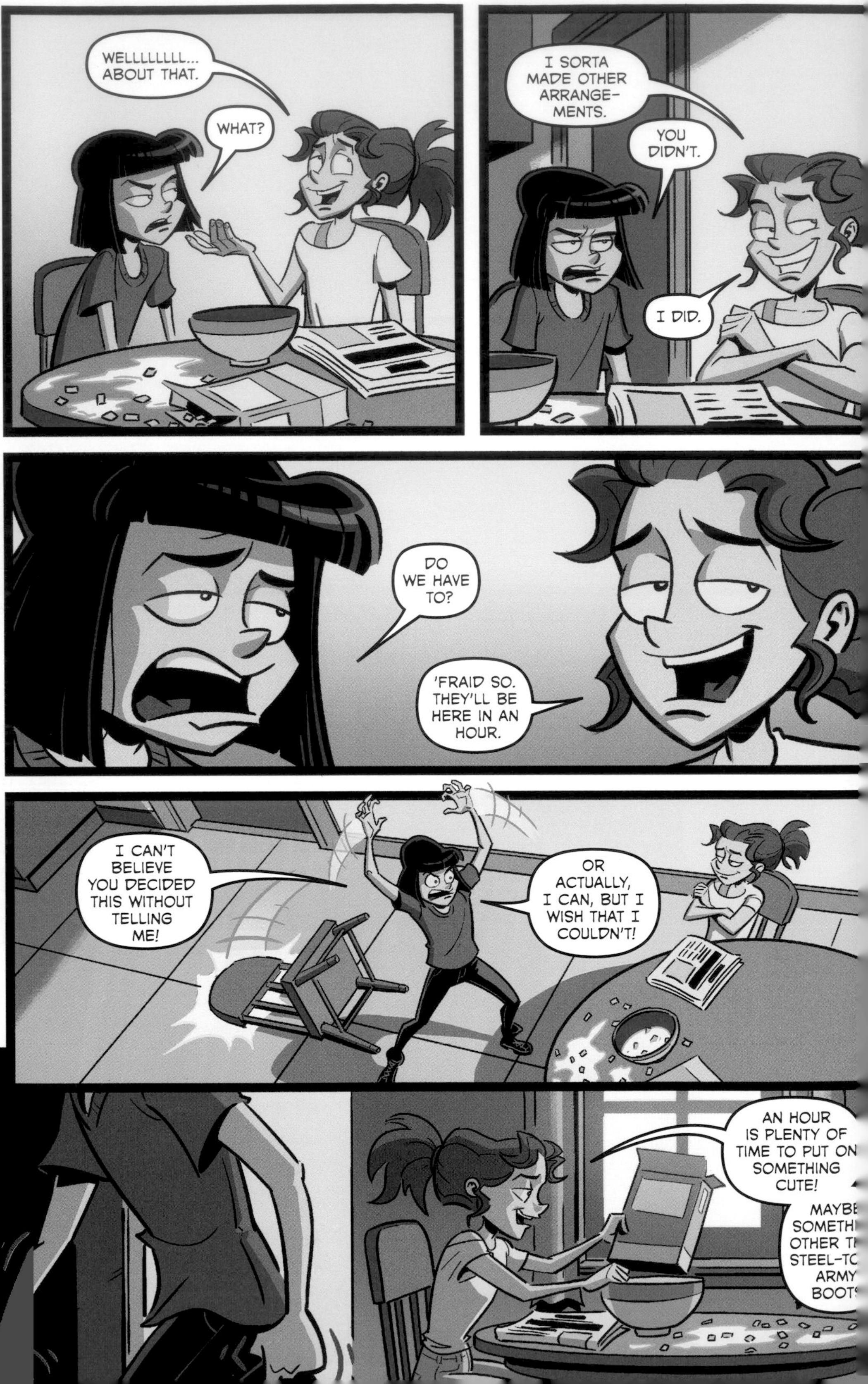
WELLLLLLLL... ABOUT THAT.
WHAT?
I SORTA MADE OTHER ARRANGE-MENTS.
YOU DIDN'T.
I DID.
DO WE HAVE TO?
'FRAID SO. THEY'LL BE HERE IN AN HOUR.
I CAN'T BELIEVE YOU DECIDED THIS WITHOUT TELLING ME!
OR ACTUALLY, I CAN, BUT I WISH THAT I COULDN'T!
AN HOUR IS PLENTY OF TIME TO PUT ON SOMETHING CUTE!

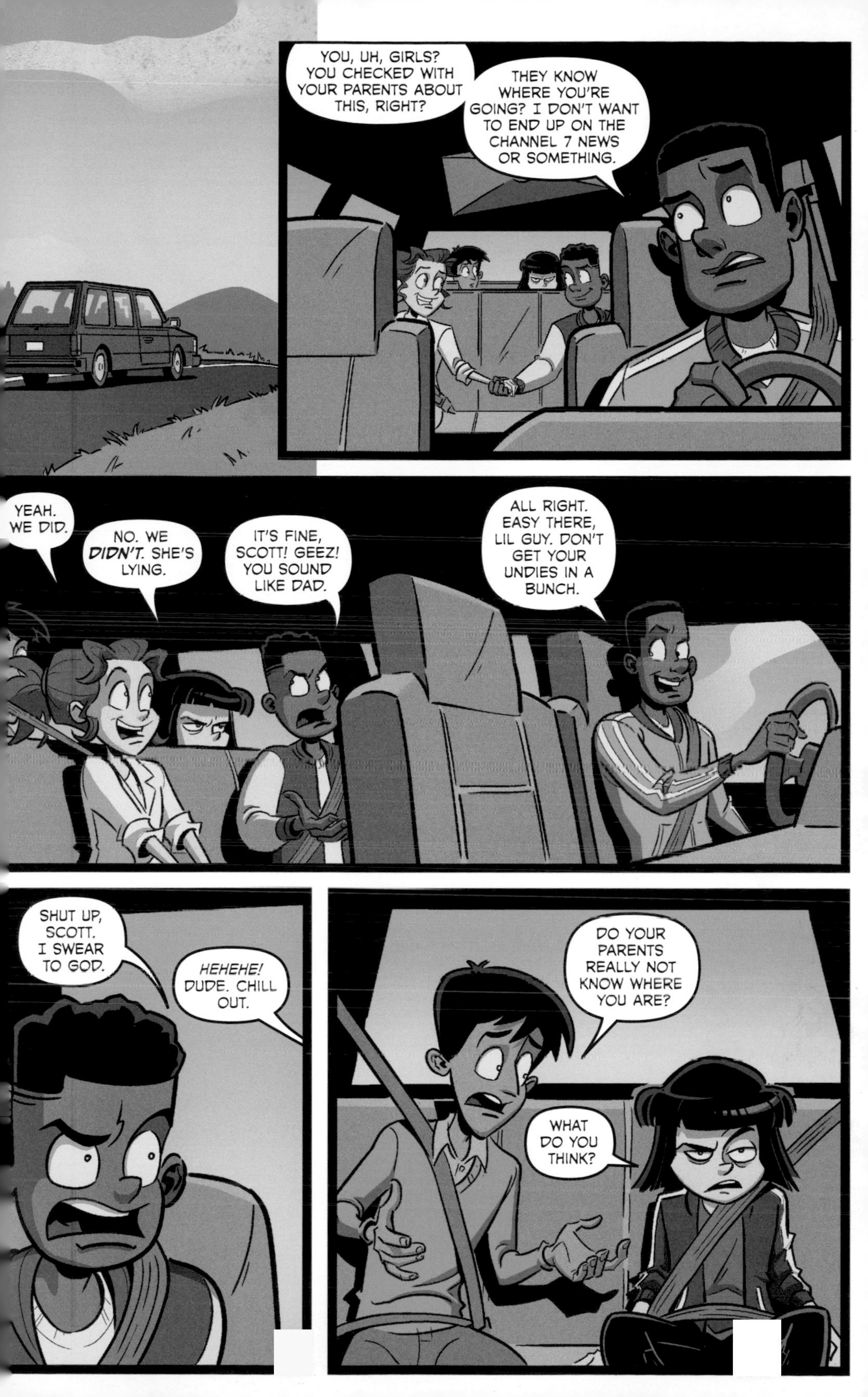
YOU, UH, GIRLS? YOU CHECKED WITH YOUR PARENTS ABOUT THIS, RIGHT?
THEY KNOW WHERE YOU'RE GOING? I DON'T WANT TO END UP ON THE CHANNEL 7 NEWS OR SOMETHING.
YEAH. WE DID.
NO. WE *DIDN'T*. SHE'S LYING.
IT'S FINE, SCOTT! GEEZ! YOU SOUND LIKE DAD.
ALL RIGHT. EASY THERE, LIL GUY. DON'T GET YOUR UNDIES IN A BUNCH.
SHUT UP, SCOTT. I SWEAR TO GOD.
HEHEHE! DUDE. CHILL OUT.
DO YOUR PARENTS REALLY NOT KNOW WHERE YOU ARE?
WHAT DO YOU THINK?

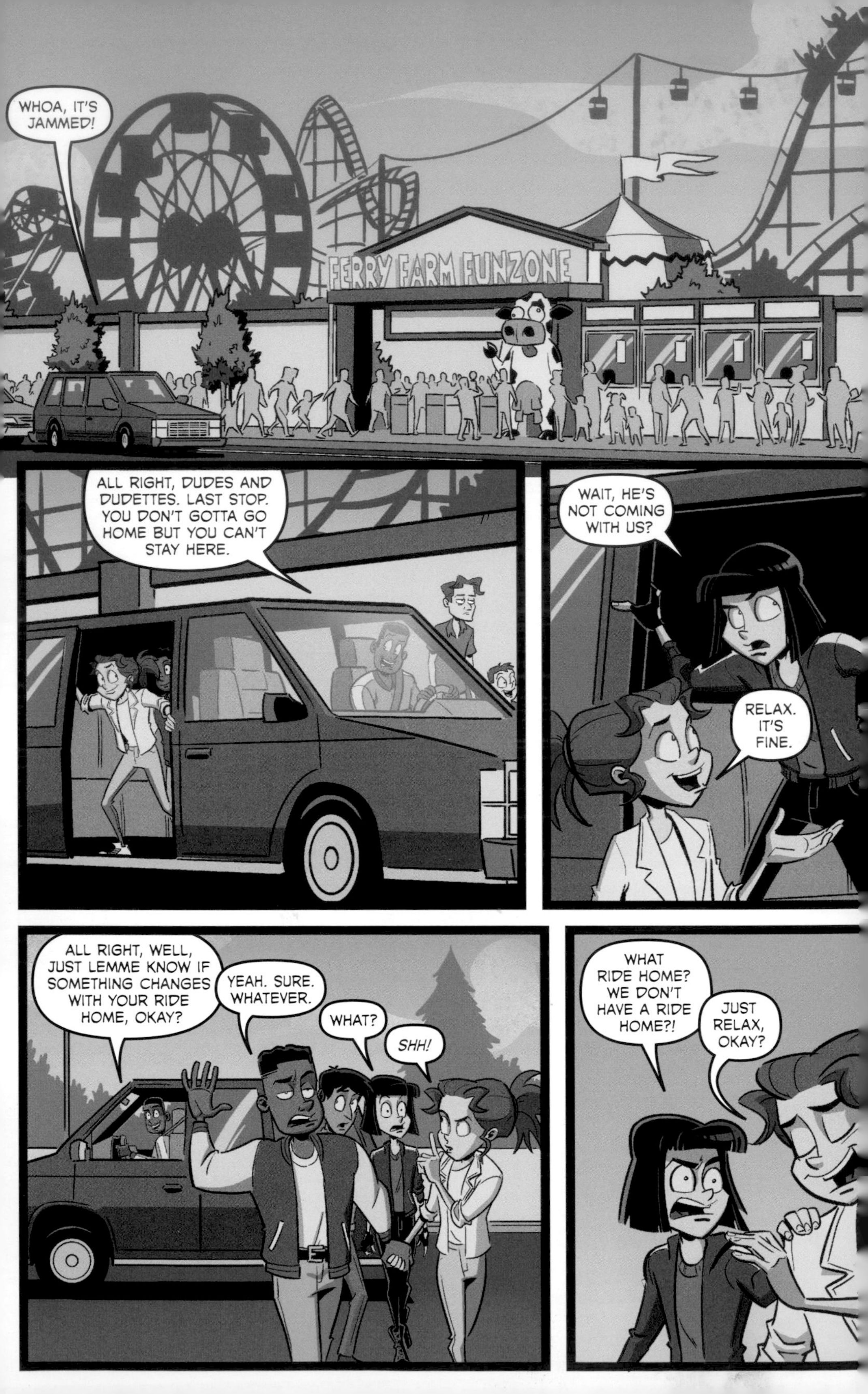
WHOA, IT'S JAMMED!
FERRY FARM FUNZONE
ALL RIGHT, DUDES AND DUDETTES. LAST STOP. YOU DON'T GOTTA GO HOME BUT YOU CAN'T STAY HERE.
WAIT, HE'S NOT COMING WITH US?
RELAX. IT'S FINE.
ALL RIGHT, WELL, JUST LEMME KNOW IF SOMETHING CHANGES WITH YOUR RIDE HOME, OKAY?
YEAH. SURE. WHATEVER.
WHAT?
SHH!
WHAT RIDE HOME? WE DON'T HAVE A RIDE HOME?!
JUST RELAX, OKAY?

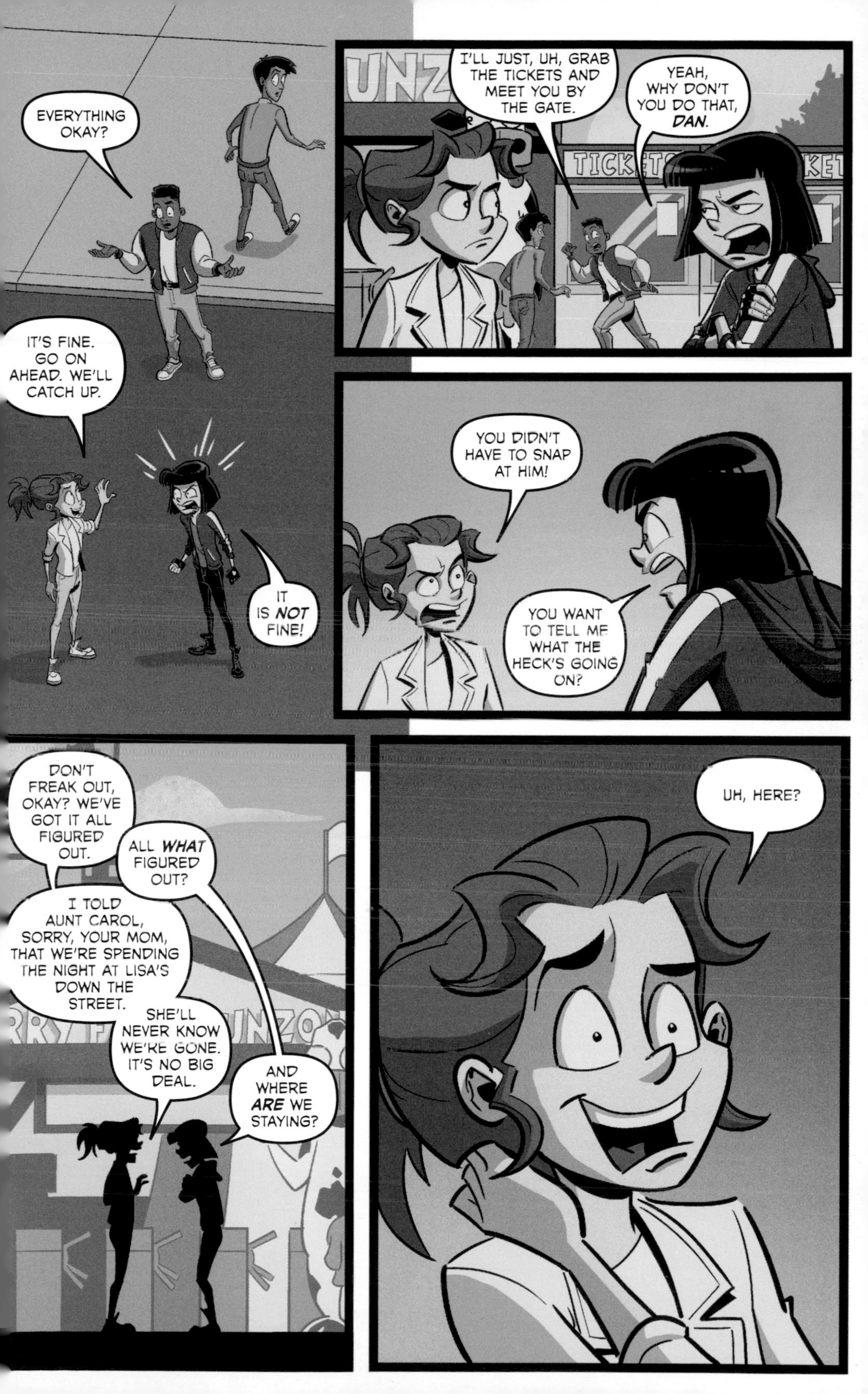
EVERYTHING OKAY?
I'LL JUST, UH, GRAB THE TICKETS AND MEET YOU BY THE GATE.
YEAH, WHY DON'T YOU DO THAT, ***DAN***.
IT'S FINE. GO ON AHEAD. WE'LL CATCH UP.
IT IS ***NOT*** FINE!
YOU DIDN'T HAVE TO SNAP AT HIM!
YOU WANT TO TELL ME WHAT THE HECK'S GOING ON?
DON'T FREAK OUT, OKAY? WE'VE GOT IT ALL FIGURED OUT.
ALL ***WHAT*** FIGURED OUT?
I TOLD AUNT CAROL, SORRY, YOUR MOM, THAT WE'RE SPENDING THE NIGHT AT LISA'S DOWN THE STREET.
SHE'LL NEVER KNOW WE'RE GONE. IT'S NO BIG DEAL.
AND WHERE ***ARE*** WE STAYING?
UH, HERE?

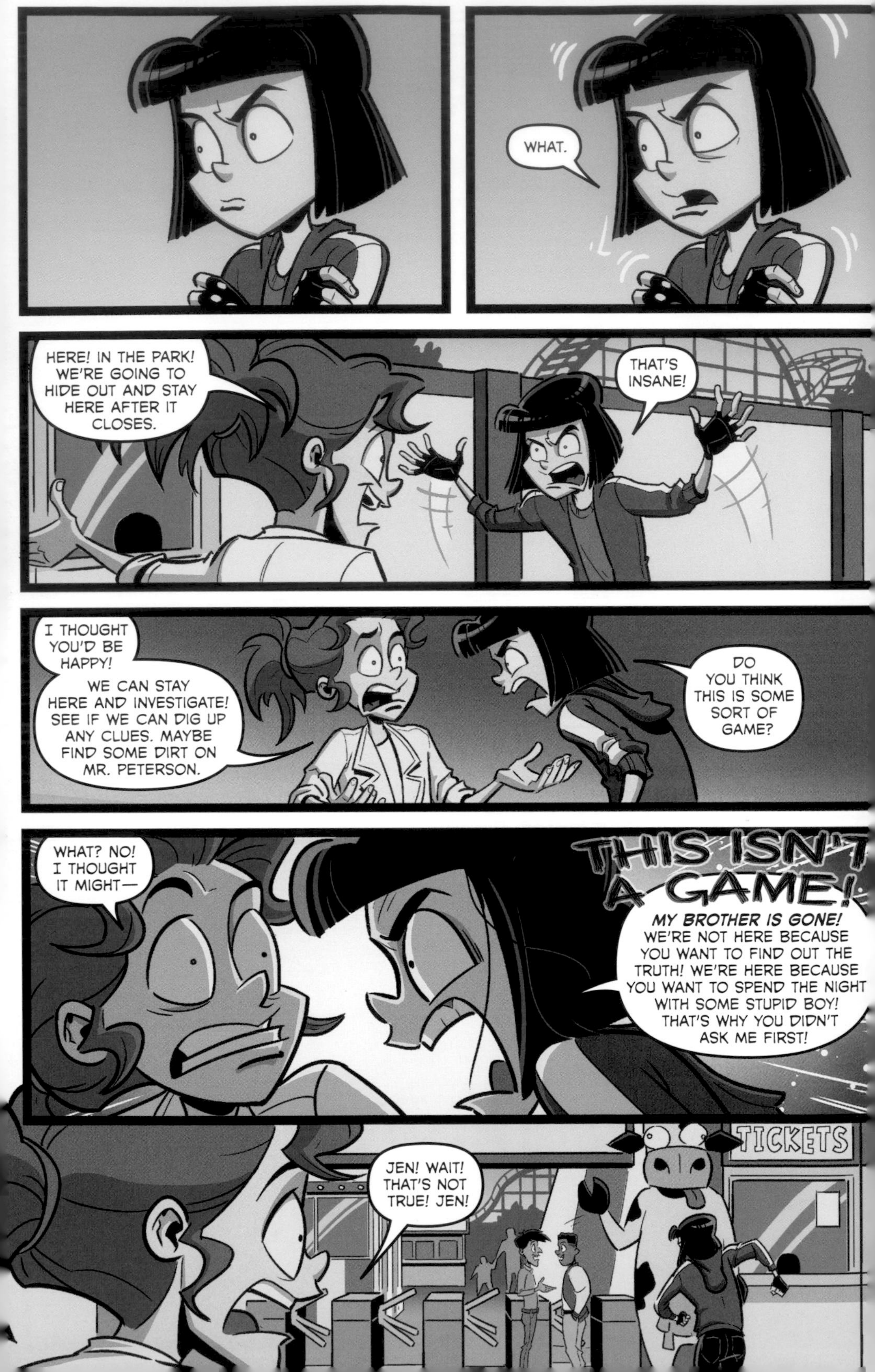
WHAT.
HERE! IN THE PARK! WE'RE GOING TO HIDE OUT AND STAY HERE AFTER IT CLOSES.
THAT'S INSANE!
I THOUGHT YOU'D BE HAPPY!
WE CAN STAY HERE AND INVESTIGATE! SEE IF WE CAN DIG UP ANY CLUES. MAYBE FIND SOME DIRT ON MR. PETERSON.
DO YOU THINK THIS IS SOME SORT OF GAME?
WHAT? NO! I THOUGHT IT MIGHT—
THIS ISN'T A GAME!
MY BROTHER IS GONE! WE'RE NOT HERE BECAUSE YOU WANT TO FIND OUT THE TRUTH! WE'RE HERE BECAUSE YOU WANT TO SPEND THE NIGHT WITH SOME STUPID BOY! THAT'S WHY YOU DIDN'T ASK ME FIRST!
TICKETS
JEN! WAIT! THAT'S NOT TRUE! JEN!

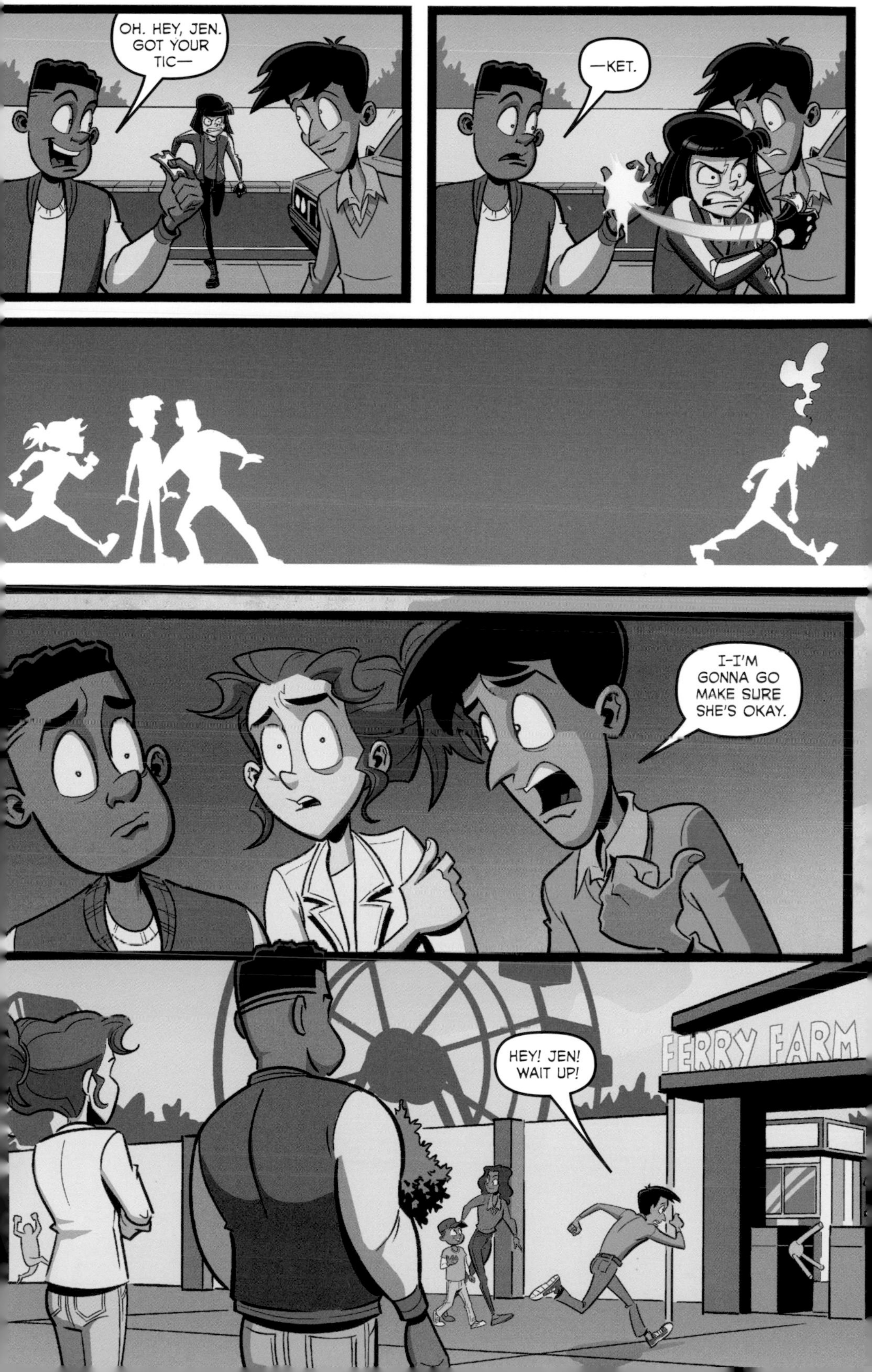
OH. HEY, JEN. GOT YOUR TIC—
—KET.
I-I'M GONNA GO MAKE SURE SHE'S OKAY.
FERRY FARM
HEY! JEN! WAIT UP!

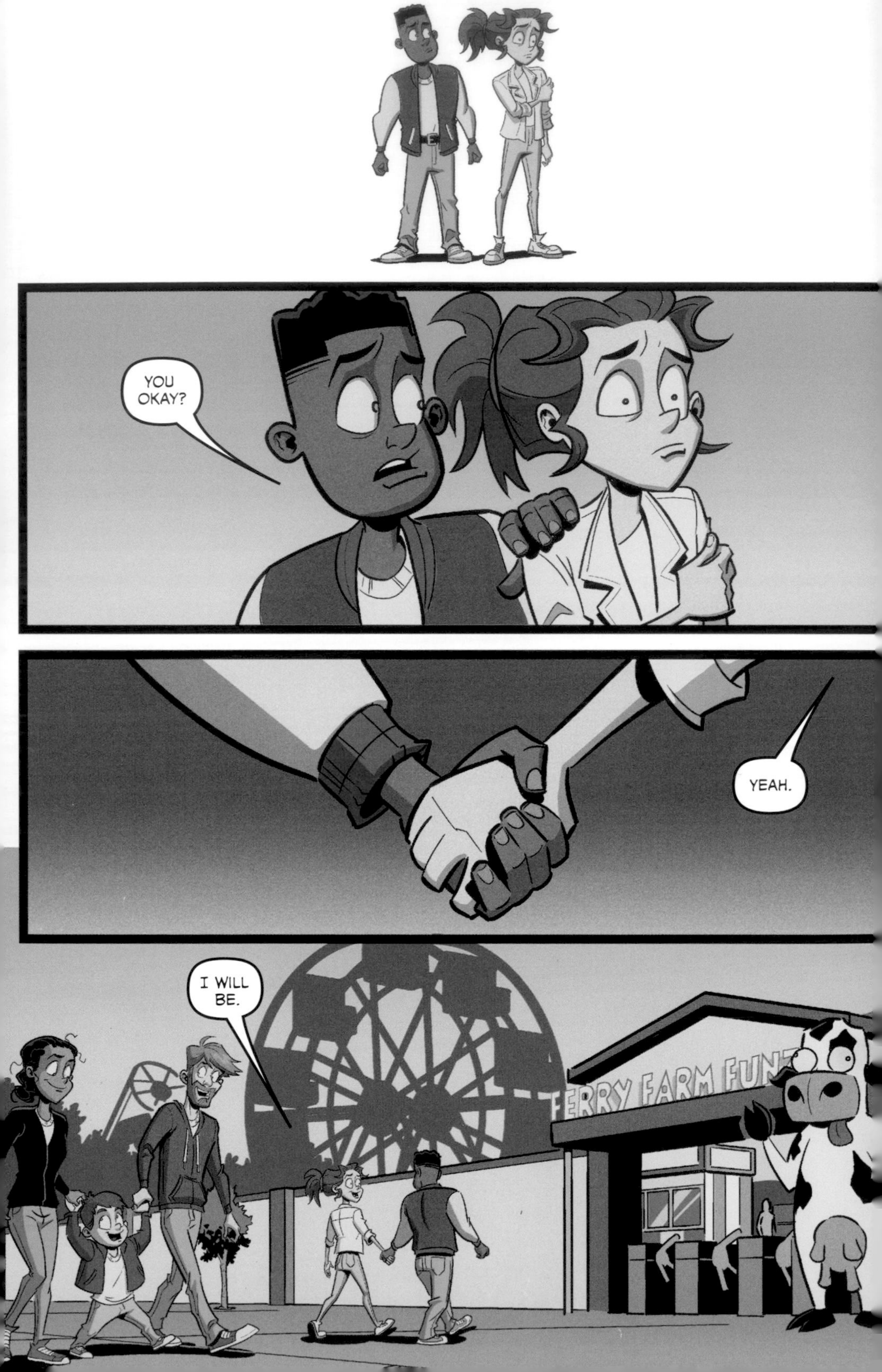
YOU OKAY?
YEAH.
I WILL BE.
FERRY FARM FUN

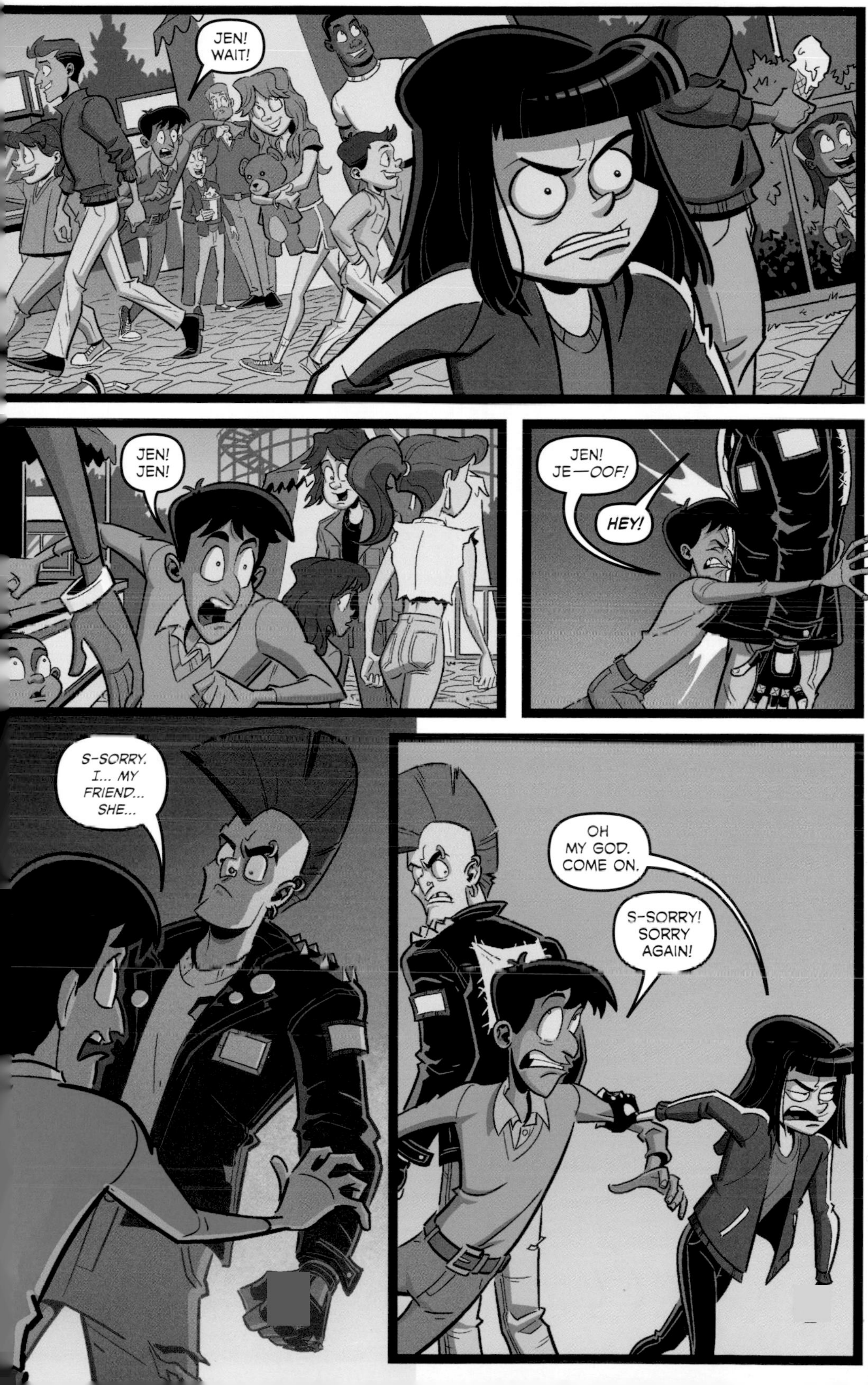
JEN! WAIT!
JEN! JEN!
JEN! JE—OOF!
HEY!
S-SORRY. I... MY FRIEND... SHE...
OH MY GOD. COME ON.
S-SORRY! SORRY AGAIN!

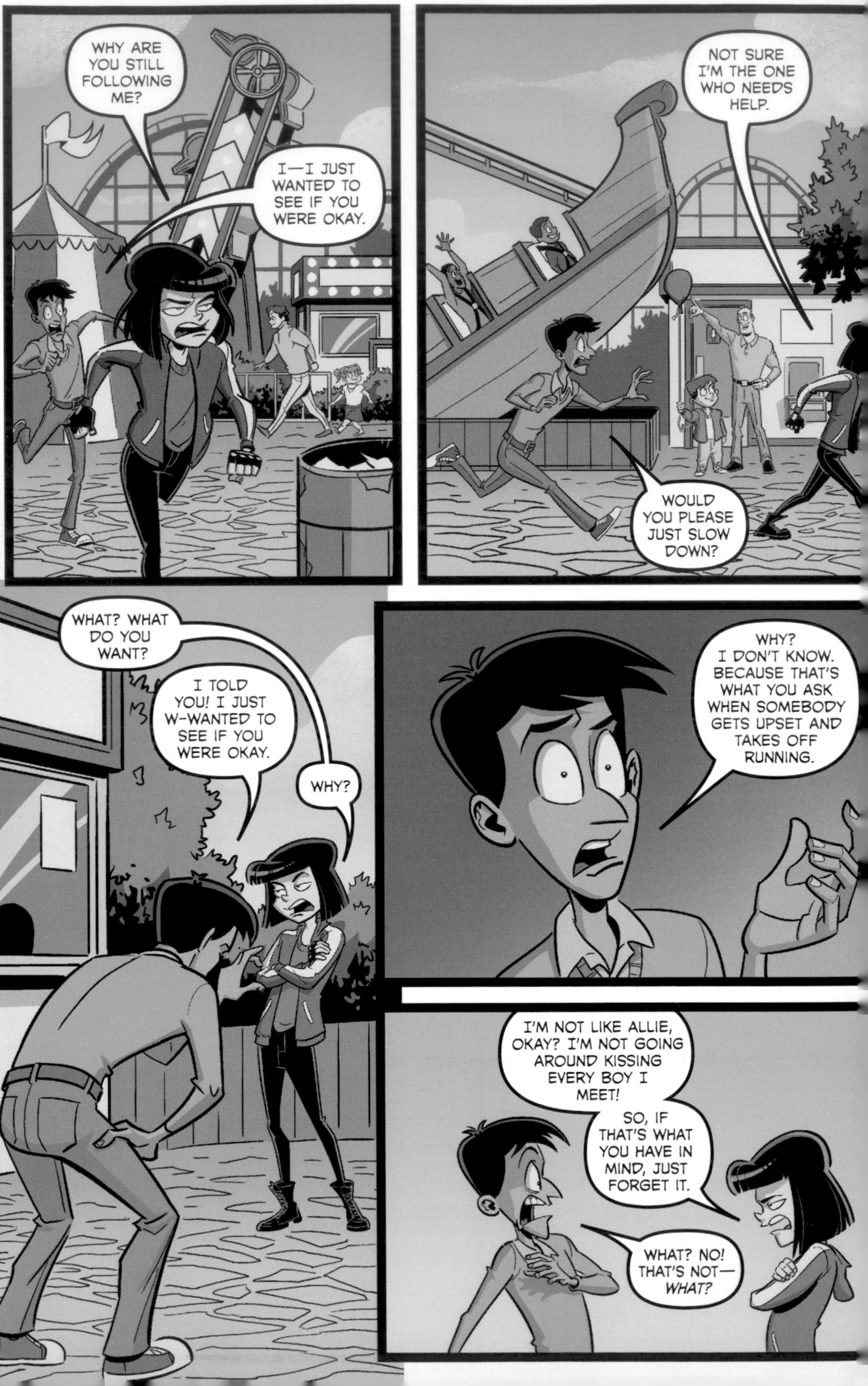
WHY ARE YOU STILL FOLLOWING ME?
I—I JUST WANTED TO SEE IF YOU WERE OKAY.
NOT SURE I'M THE ONE WHO NEEDS HELP.
WOULD YOU PLEASE JUST SLOW DOWN?
WHAT? WHAT DO YOU WANT?
I TOLD YOU! I JUST W-WANTED TO SEE IF YOU WERE OKAY.
WHY?
WHY? I DON'T KNOW. BECAUSE THAT'S WHAT YOU ASK WHEN SOMEBODY GETS UPSET AND TAKES OFF RUNNING.
I'M NOT LIKE ALLIE, OKAY? I'M NOT GOING AROUND KISSING EVERY BOY I MEET!
SO, IF THAT'S WHAT YOU HAVE IN MIND, JUST FORGET IT.
WHAT? NO! THAT'S NOT—*WHAT?*

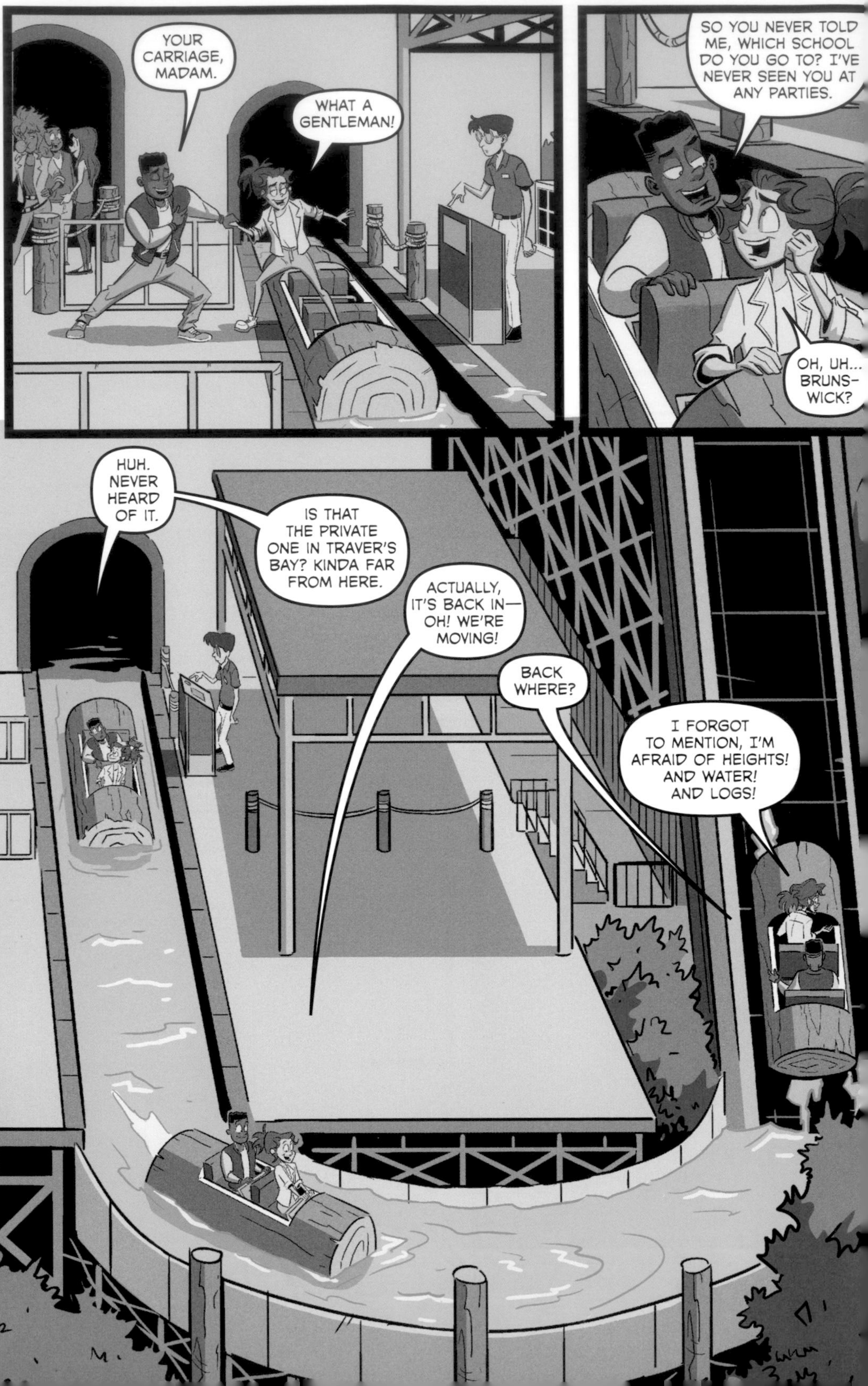

YOUR CARRIAGE, MADAM.
WHAT A GENTLEMAN!
SO YOU NEVER TOLD ME, WHICH SCHOOL DO YOU GO TO? I'VE NEVER SEEN YOU AT ANY PARTIES.
OH, UH... BRUNS-WICK?
HUH. NEVER HEARD OF IT.
IS THAT THE PRIVATE ONE IN TRAVER'S BAY? KINDA FAR FROM HERE.
ACTUALLY, IT'S BACK IN— OH! WE'RE MOVING!
BACK WHERE?
I FORGOT TO MENTION, I'M AFRAID OF HEIGHTS! AND WATER! AND LOGS!

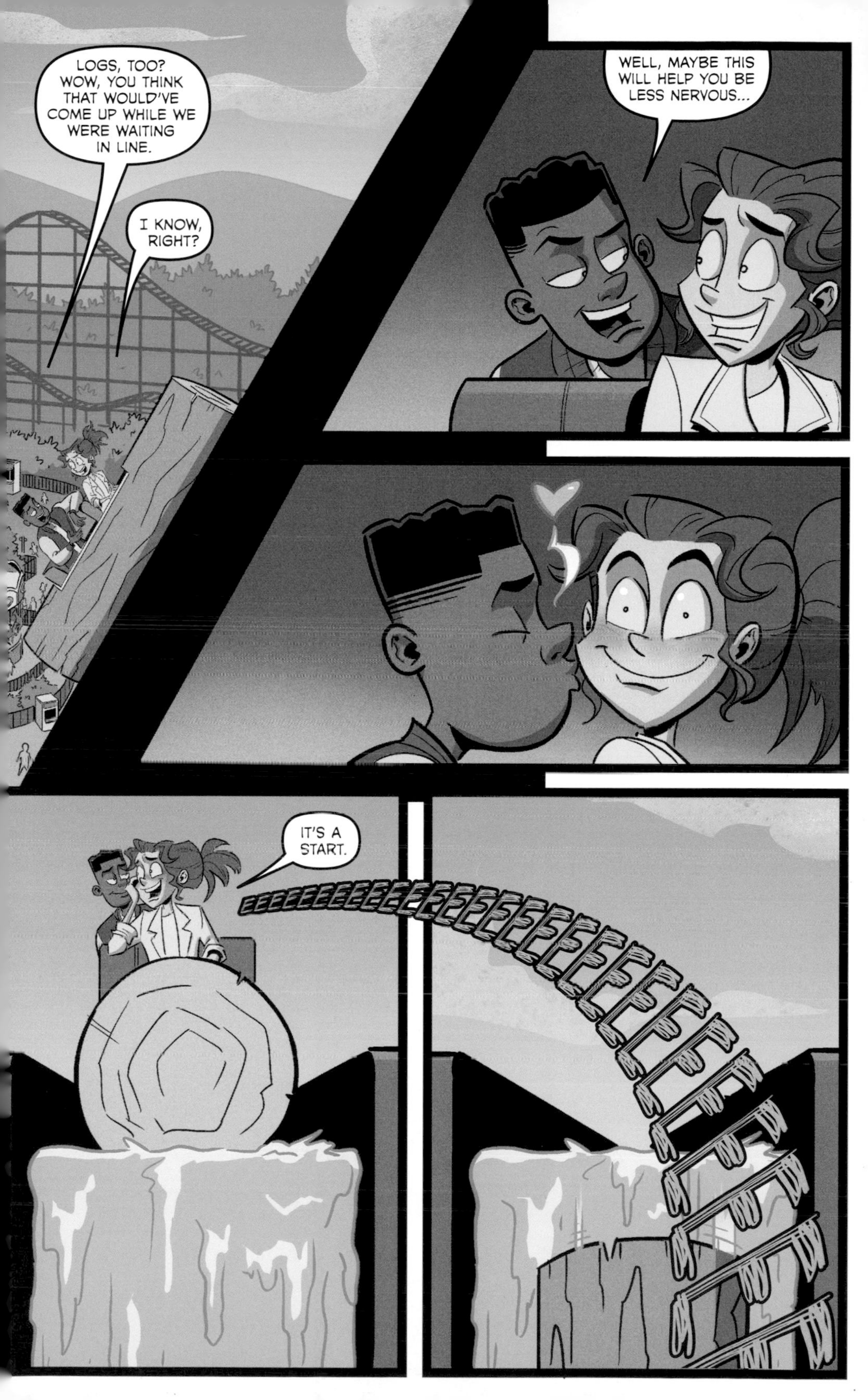
LOGS, TOO? WOW, YOU THINK THAT WOULD'VE COME UP WHILE WE WERE WAITING IN LINE.
I KNOW, RIGHT?
WELL, MAYBE THIS WILL HELP YOU BE LESS NERVOUS...
IT'S A START.

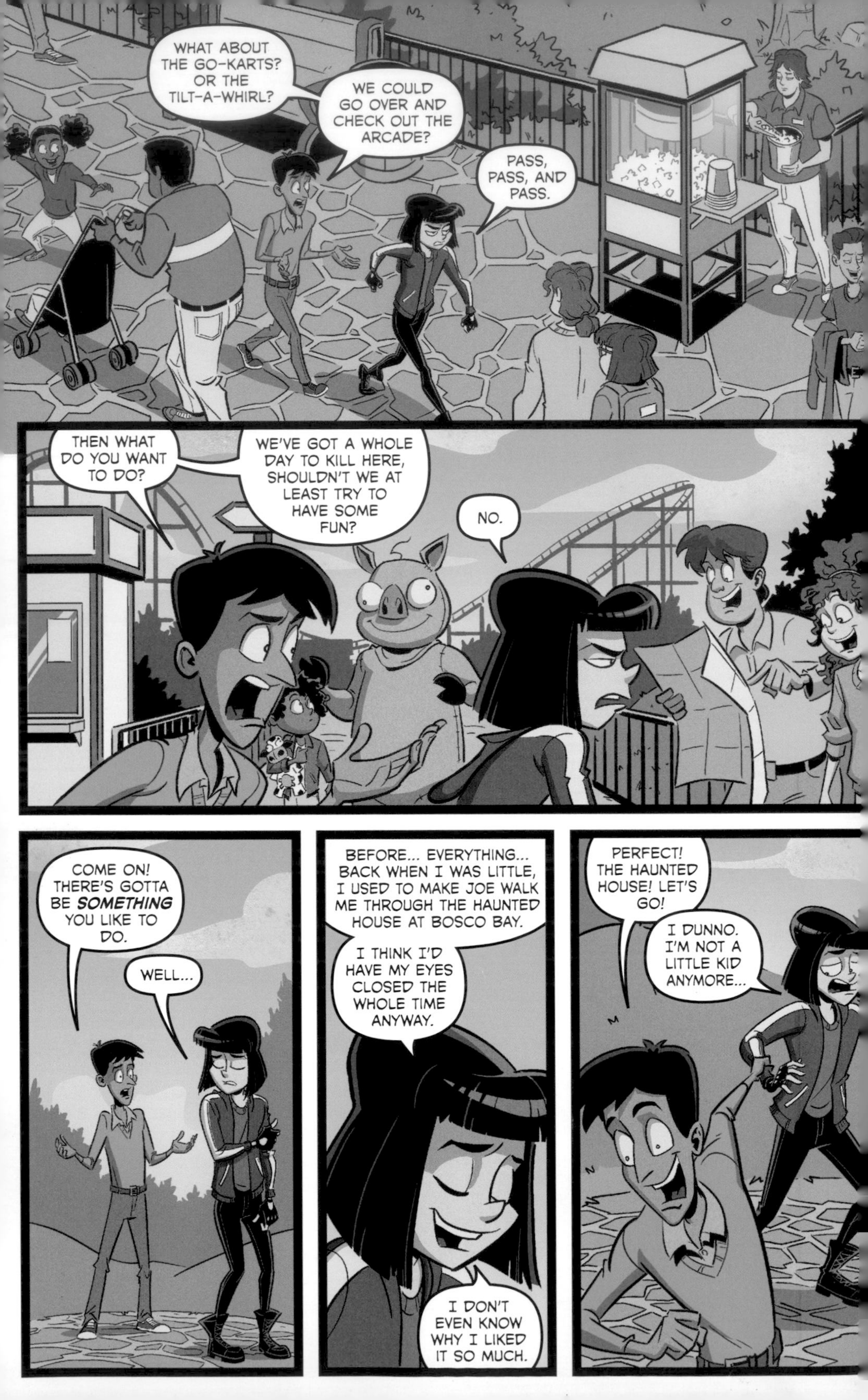
WHAT ABOUT THE GO-KARTS? OR THE TILT-A-WHIRL?
WE COULD GO OVER AND CHECK OUT THE ARCADE?
PASS, PASS, AND PASS.
THEN WHAT DO YOU WANT TO DO?
WE'VE GOT A WHOLE DAY TO KILL HERE, SHOULDN'T WE AT LEAST TRY TO HAVE SOME FUN?
NO.
COME ON! THERE'S GOTTA BE *SOMETHING* YOU LIKE TO DO.
WELL...
BEFORE... EVERYTHING... BACK WHEN I WAS LITTLE, I USED TO MAKE JOE WALK ME THROUGH THE HAUNTED HOUSE AT BOSCO BAY.
I THINK I'D HAVE MY EYES CLOSED THE WHOLE TIME ANYWAY.
I DON'T EVEN KNOW WHY I LIKED IT SO MUCH.
PERFECT! THE HAUNTED HOUSE! LET'S GO!
I DUNNO. I'M NOT A LITTLE KID ANYMORE...

UGH. THEY MUST'VE GOTTEN A GREAT DEAL ON SPIDERWEBS.

NICE TRY.

I CAN'T BELIEVE THIS STUFF USED TO SCARE ME.

HA, YEAH...

IT'S SOME SORT OF MAZE.

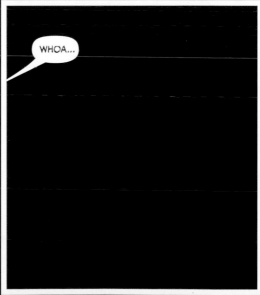

WHOA...

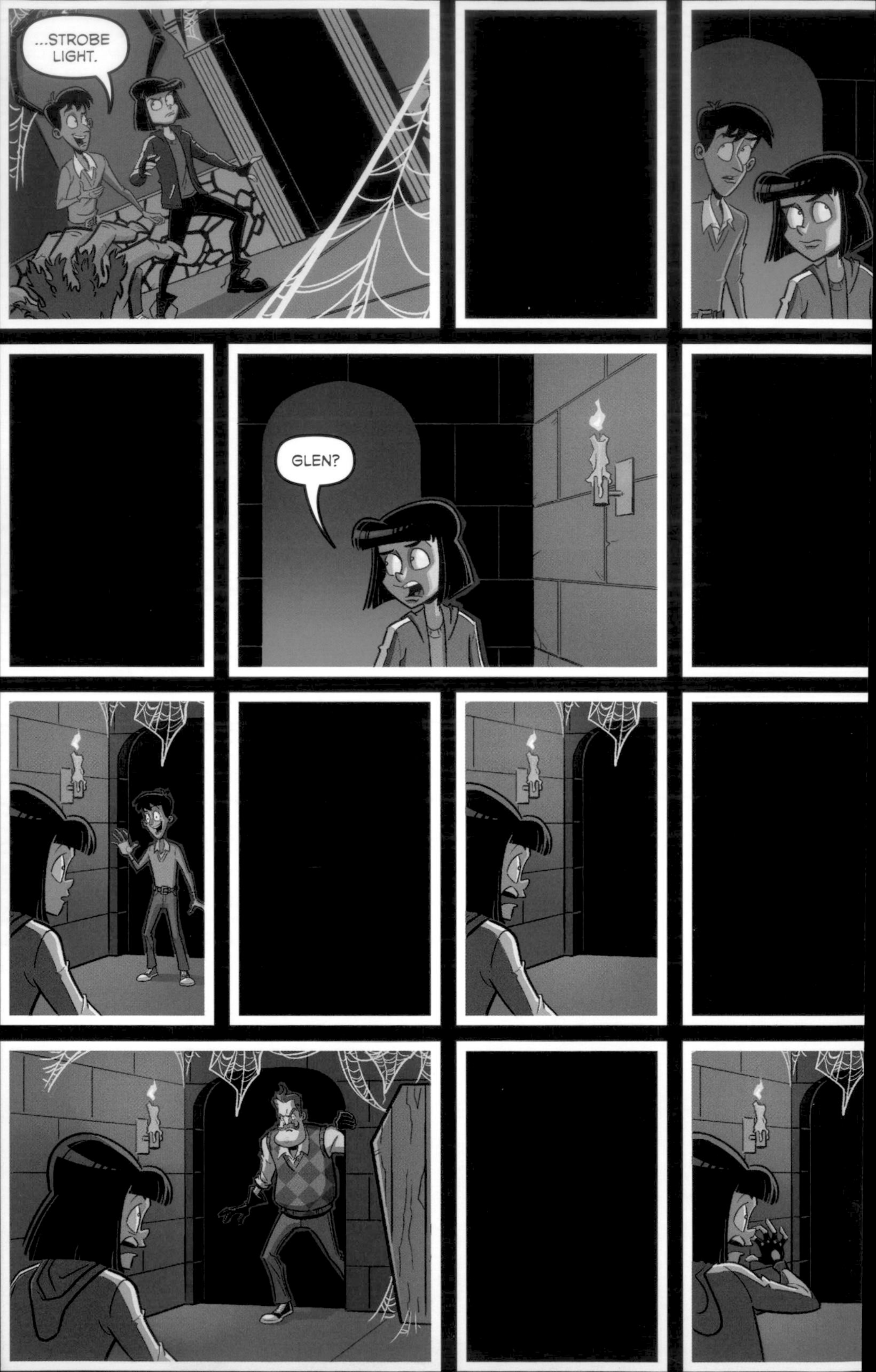
...STROBE LIGHT.
GLEN?

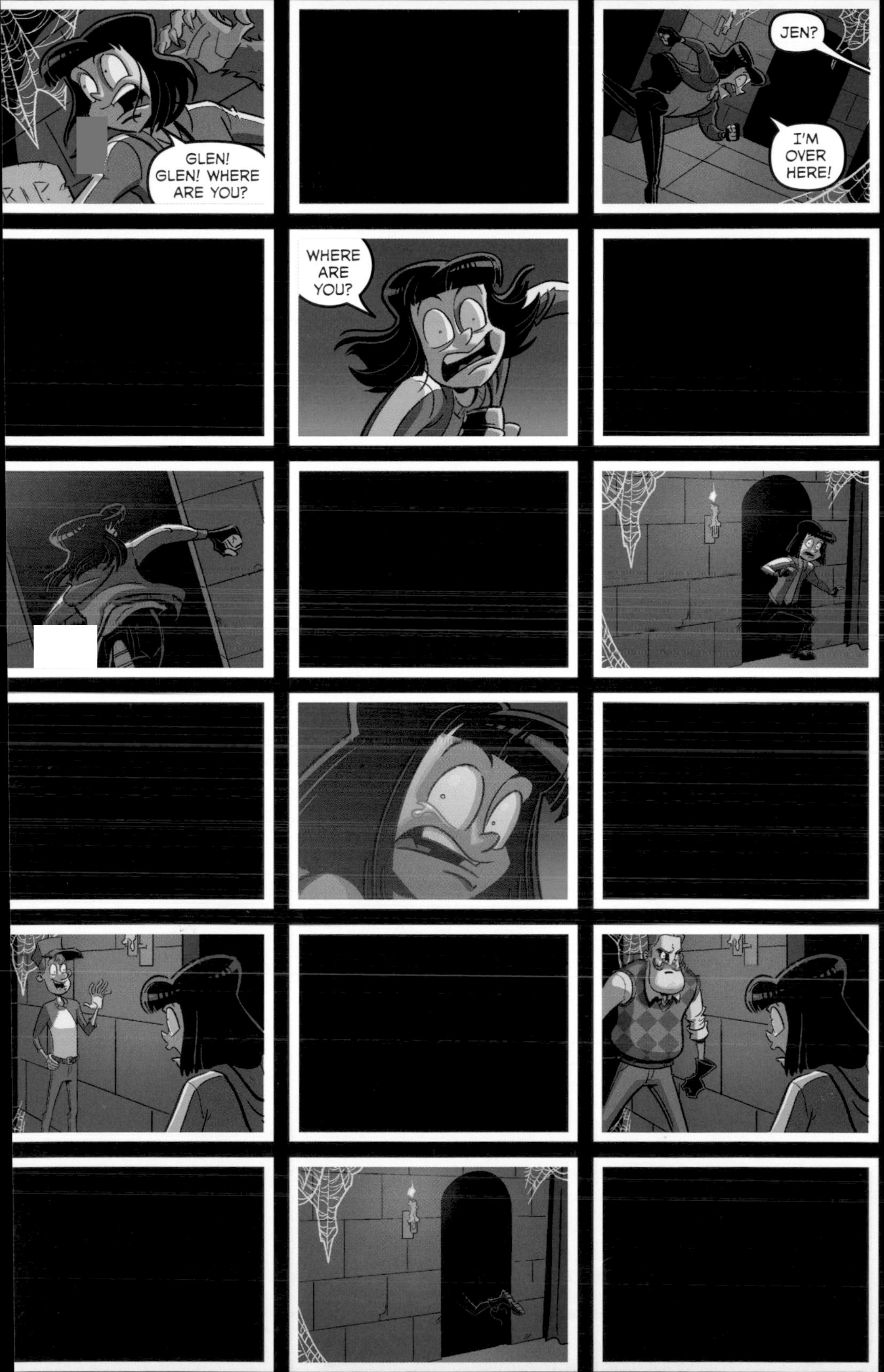
GLEN! GLEN! WHERE ARE YOU?
JEN?
I'M OVER HERE!
WHERE ARE YOU?

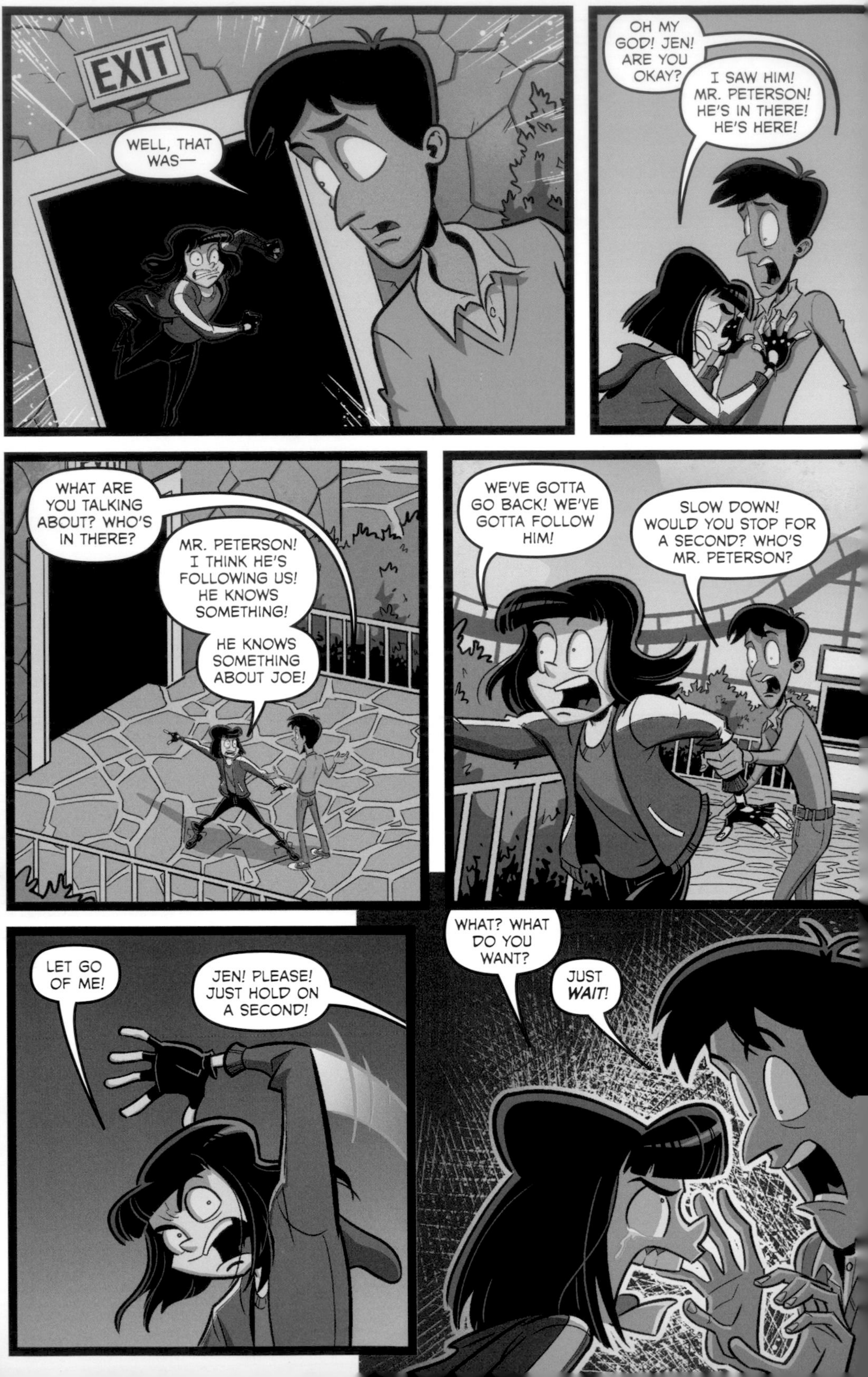
EXIT
WELL, THAT WAS—
OH MY GOD! JEN! ARE YOU OKAY?
I SAW HIM! MR. PETERSON! HE'S IN THERE! HE'S HERE!
WHAT ARE YOU TALKING ABOUT? WHO'S IN THERE?
MR. PETERSON! I THINK HE'S FOLLOWING US! HE KNOWS SOMETHING!
HE KNOWS SOMETHING ABOUT JOE!
WE'VE GOTTA GO BACK! WE'VE GOTTA FOLLOW HIM!
SLOW DOWN! WOULD YOU STOP FOR A SECOND? WHO'S MR. PETERSON?
LET GO OF ME!
JEN! PLEASE! JUST HOLD ON A SECOND!
WHAT? WHAT DO YOU WANT?
JUST *WAIT*!

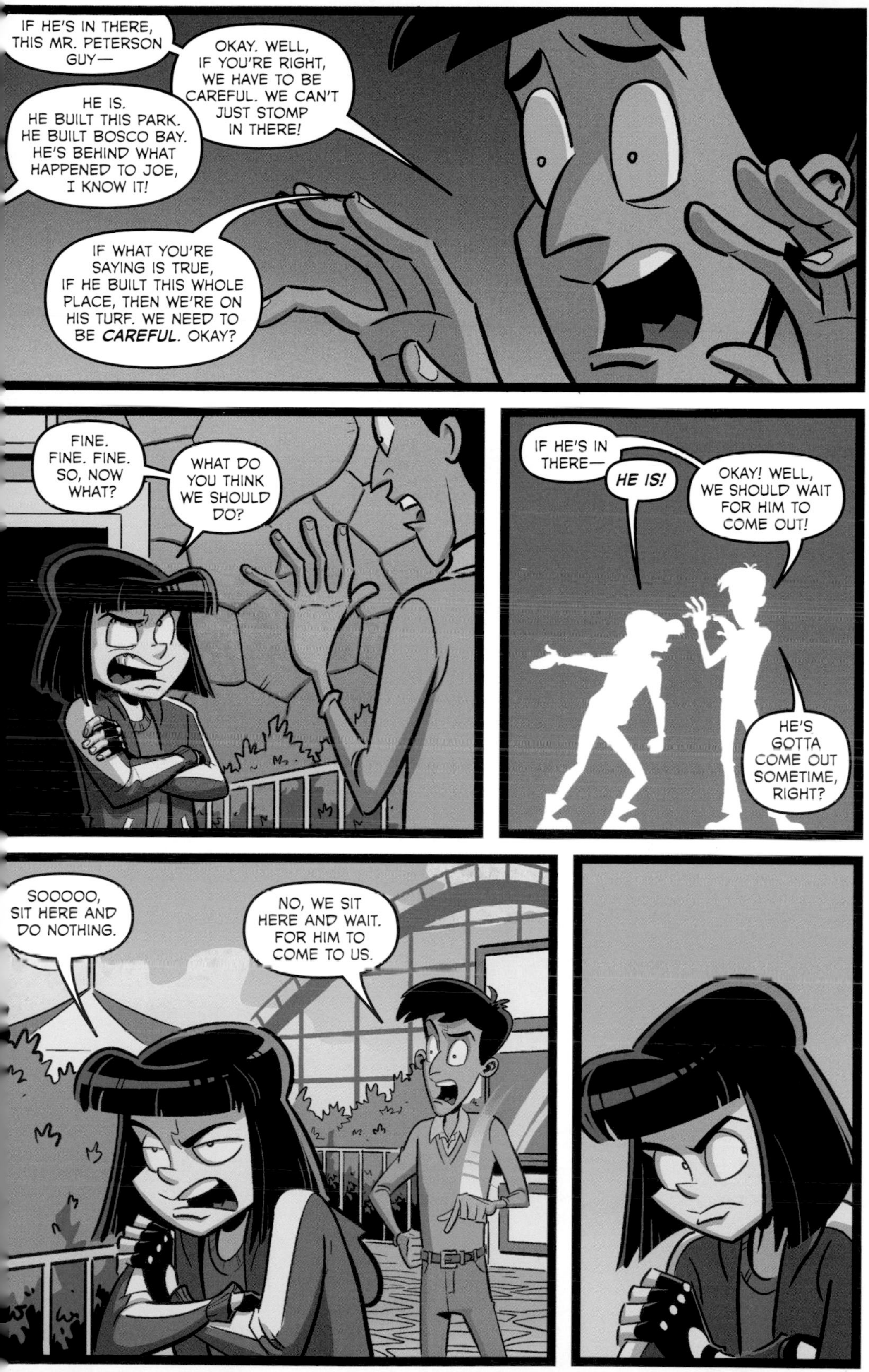

IF HE'S IN THERE, THIS MR. PETERSON GUY—
HE IS. HE BUILT THIS PARK. HE BUILT BOSCO BAY. HE'S BEHIND WHAT HAPPENED TO JOE, I KNOW IT!
OKAY. WELL, IF YOU'RE RIGHT, WE HAVE TO BE CAREFUL. WE CAN'T JUST STOMP IN THERE!
IF WHAT YOU'RE SAYING IS TRUE, IF HE BUILT THIS WHOLE PLACE, THEN WE'RE ON HIS TURF. WE NEED TO BE ***CAREFUL***. OKAY?
FINE. FINE. FINE. SO, NOW WHAT?
WHAT DO YOU THINK WE SHOULD DO?
IF HE'S IN THERE—
HE IS!
OKAY! WELL, WE SHOULD WAIT FOR HIM TO COME OUT!
HE'S GOTTA COME OUT SOMETIME, RIGHT?
SOOOOO, SIT HERE AND DO NOTHING.
NO, WE SIT HERE AND WAIT. FOR HIM TO COME TO US.

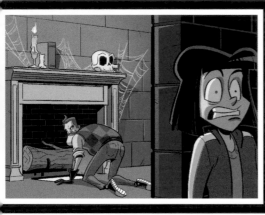

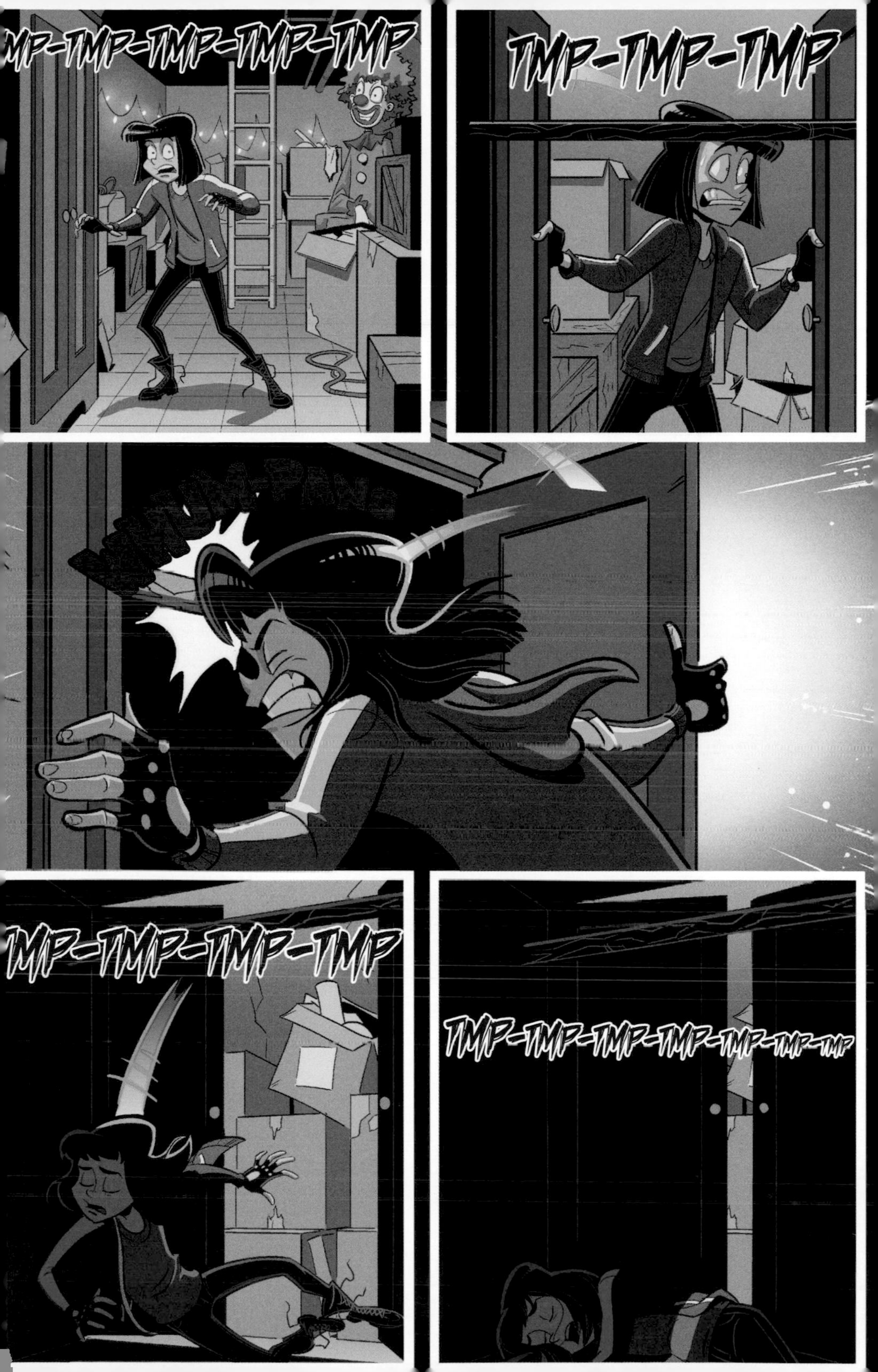
MP-TMP-TMP-TMP-TMP
TMP-TMP-TMP
TMP-TMP-TMP-TMP
TMP-TMP-TMP-TMP-TMP-TMP-TMP

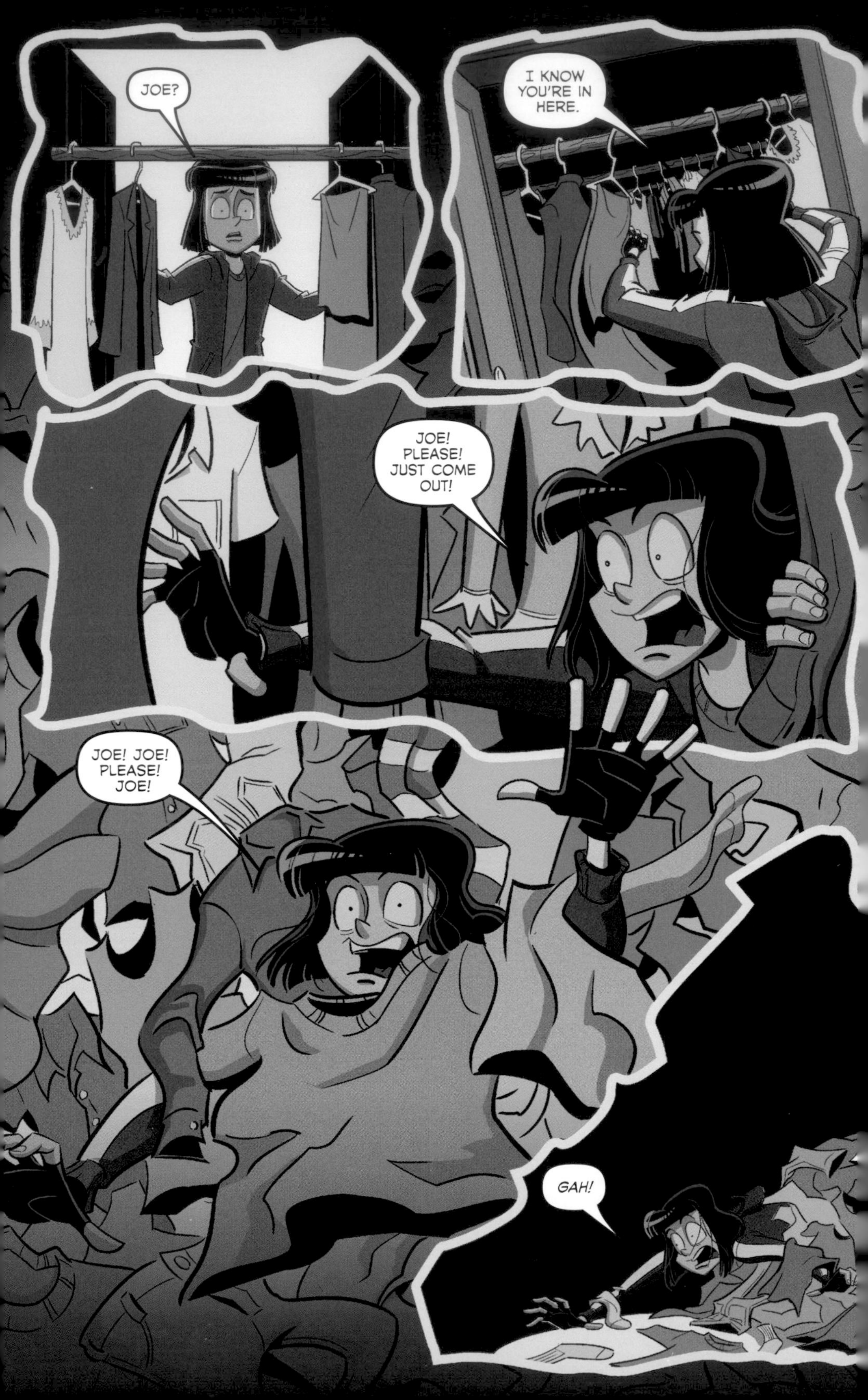
JOE?
I KNOW YOU'RE IN HERE.
JOE! PLEASE! JUST COME OUT!
JOE! JOE! PLEASE! JOE!
GAH!

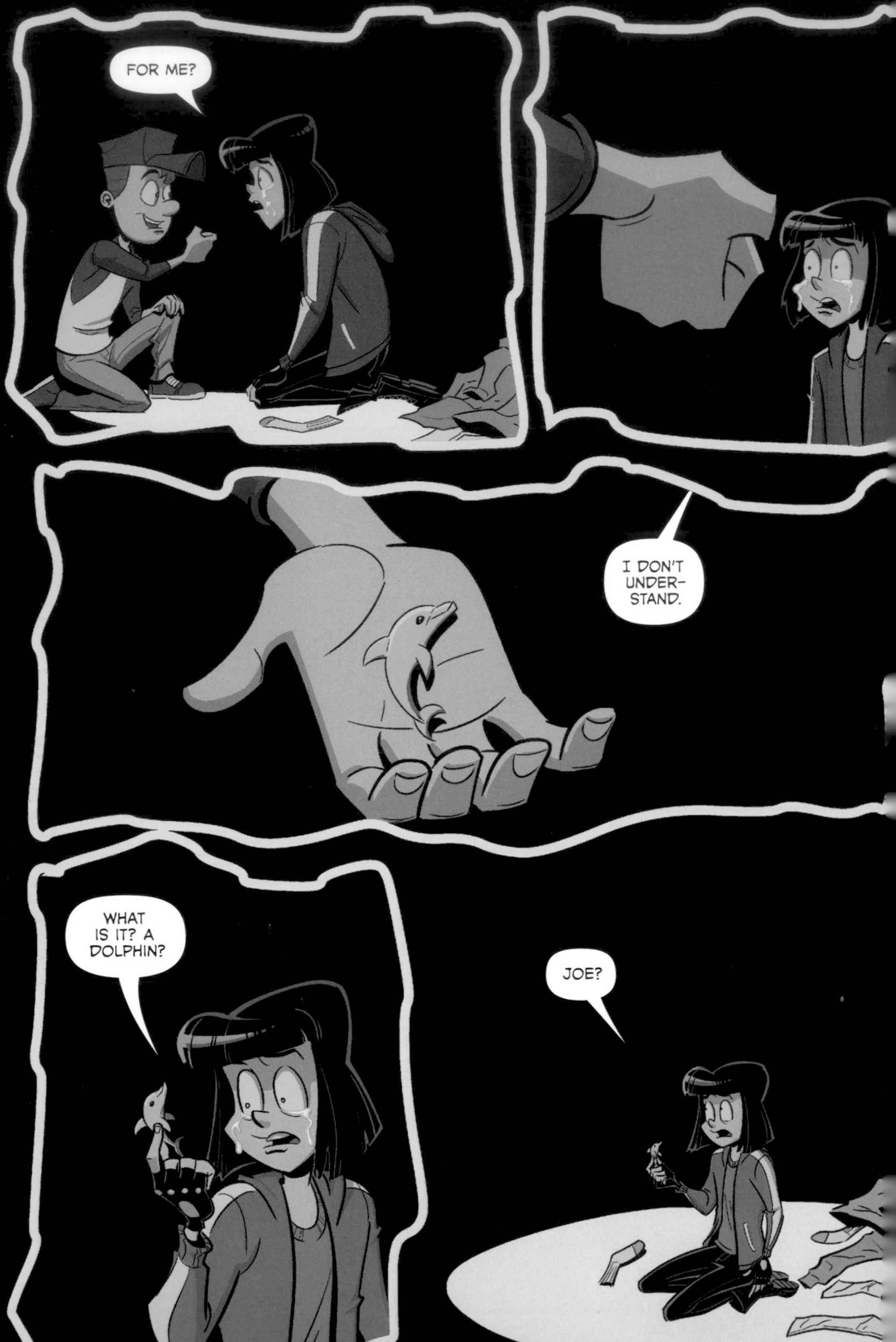
FOR ME?
I DON'T UNDER-STAND.
WHAT IS IT? A DOLPHIN?
JOE?

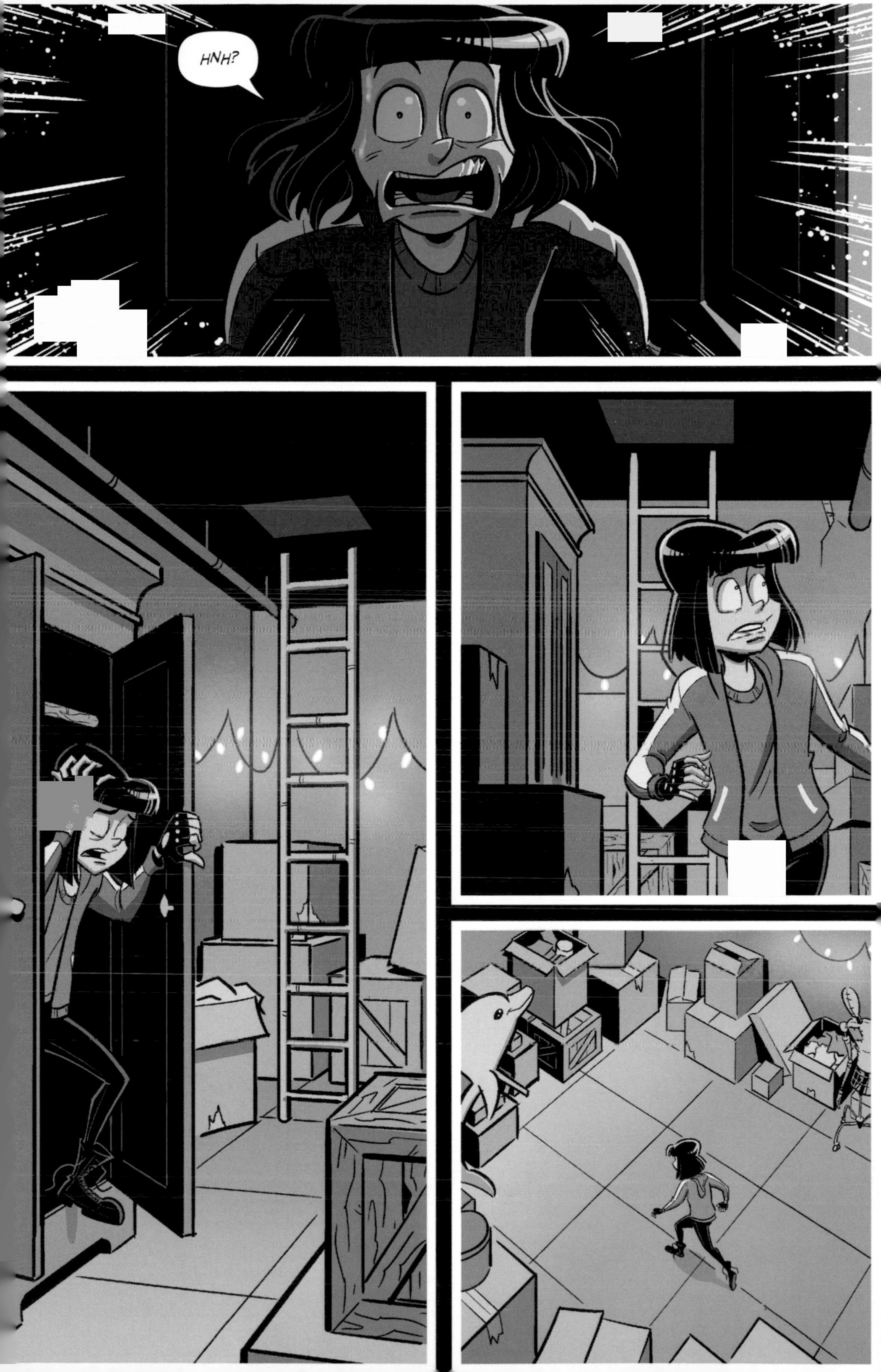
HNH?

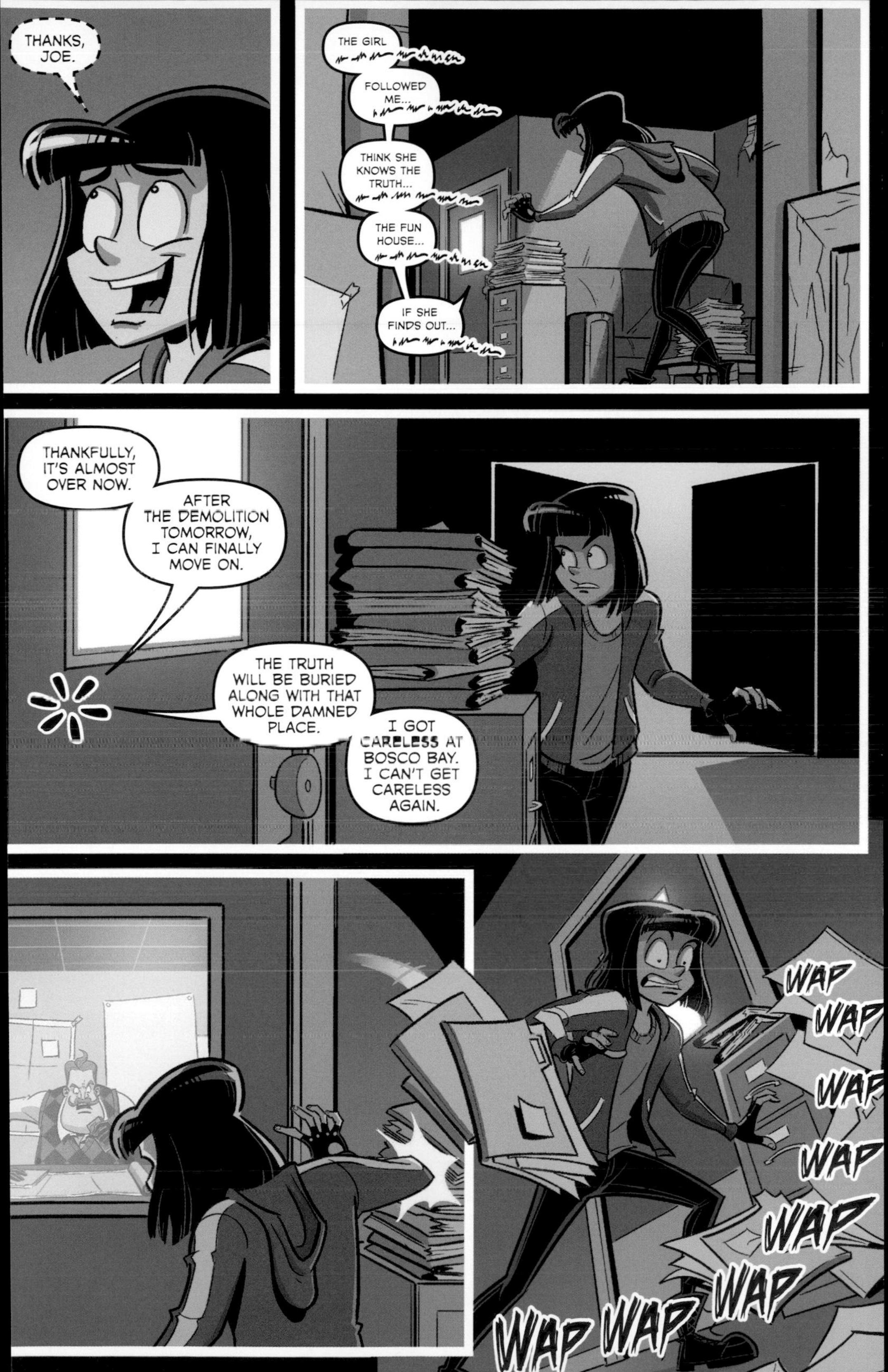
THANKS, JOE.
THE GIRL
FOLLOWED ME...
THINK SHE KNOWS THE TRUTH...
THE FUN HOUSE...
IF SHE FINDS OUT...
THANKFULLY, IT'S ALMOST OVER NOW.
AFTER THE DEMOLITION TOMORROW, I CAN FINALLY MOVE ON.
THE TRUTH WILL BE BURIED ALONG WITH THAT WHOLE DAMNED PLACE.
I GOT CARELESS AT BOSCO BAY. I CAN'T GET CARELESS AGAIN.
WAP
WAP
WAP
WAP
WAP
WAP
WAP WAP

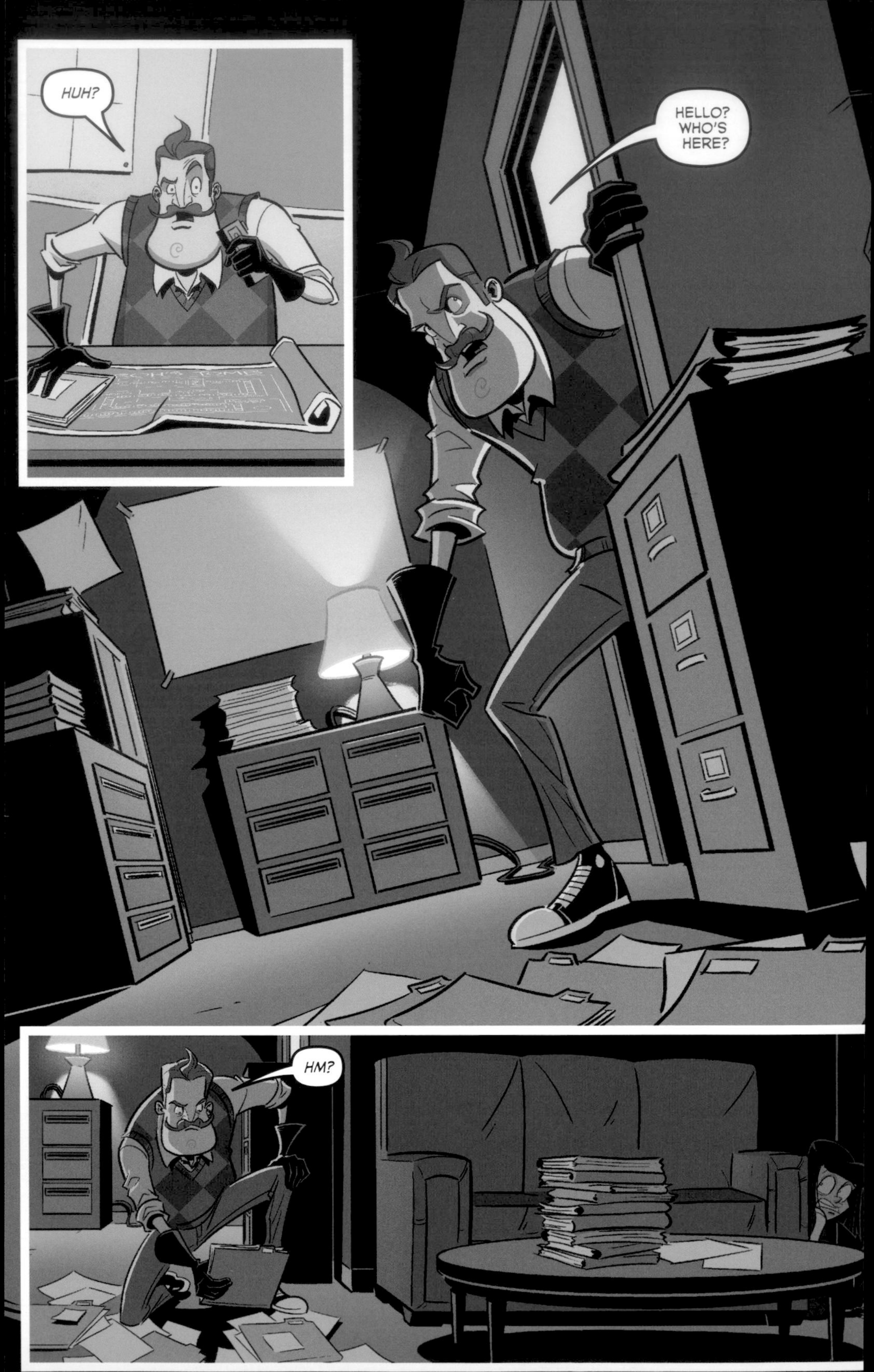
HUH?
HELLO? WHO'S HERE?
HM?

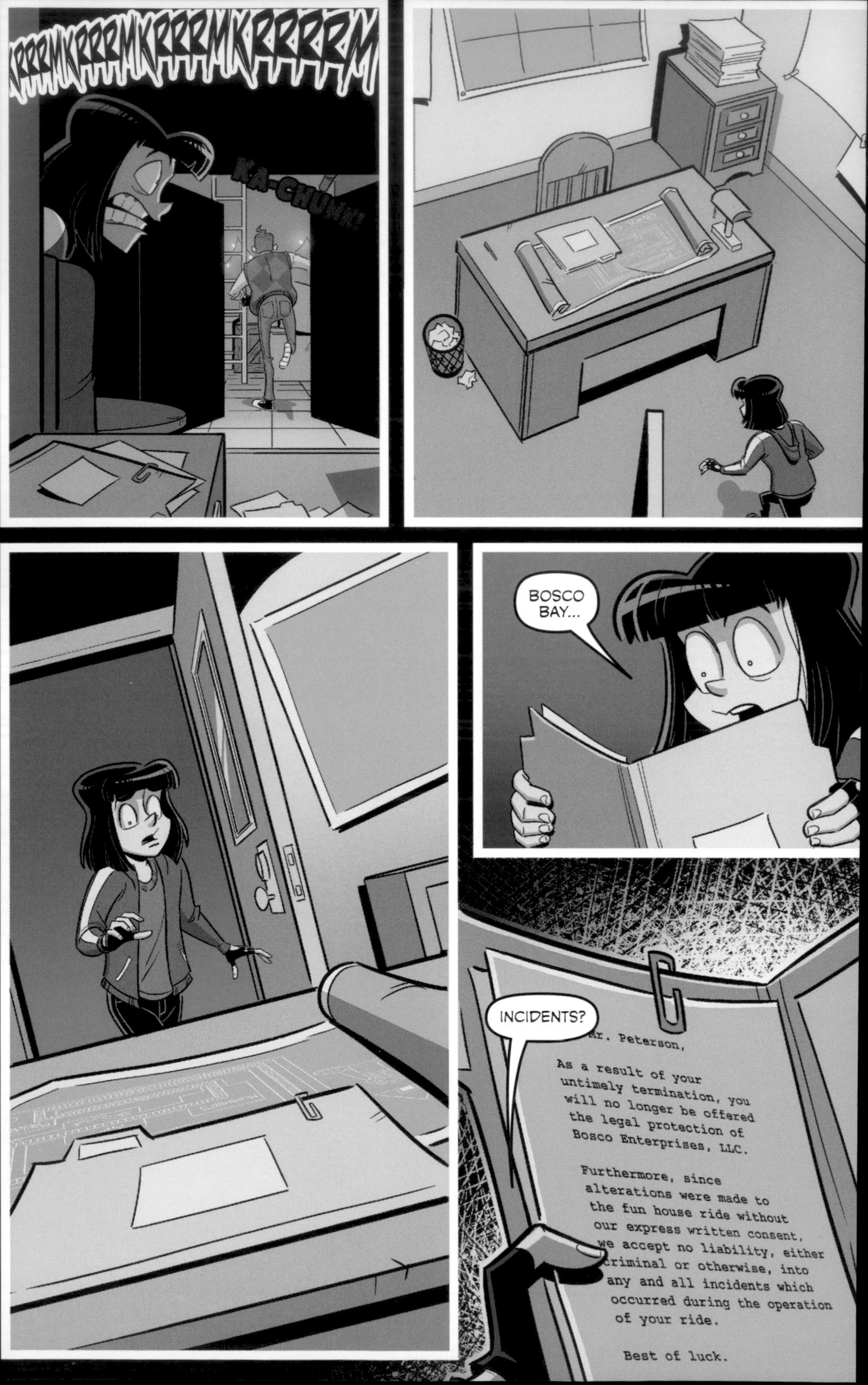
KRRRMKRRRMKRRRMKRRRRM
KA-CHUNK!
BOSCO BAY...
INCIDENTS?
Mr. Peterson,
As a result of your untimely termination, you will no longer be offered the legal protection of Bosco Enterprises, LLC.
Furthermore, since alterations were made to the fun house ride without our express written consent, we accept no liability, either criminal or otherwise, into any and all incidents which occurred during the operation of your ride.
Best of luck.

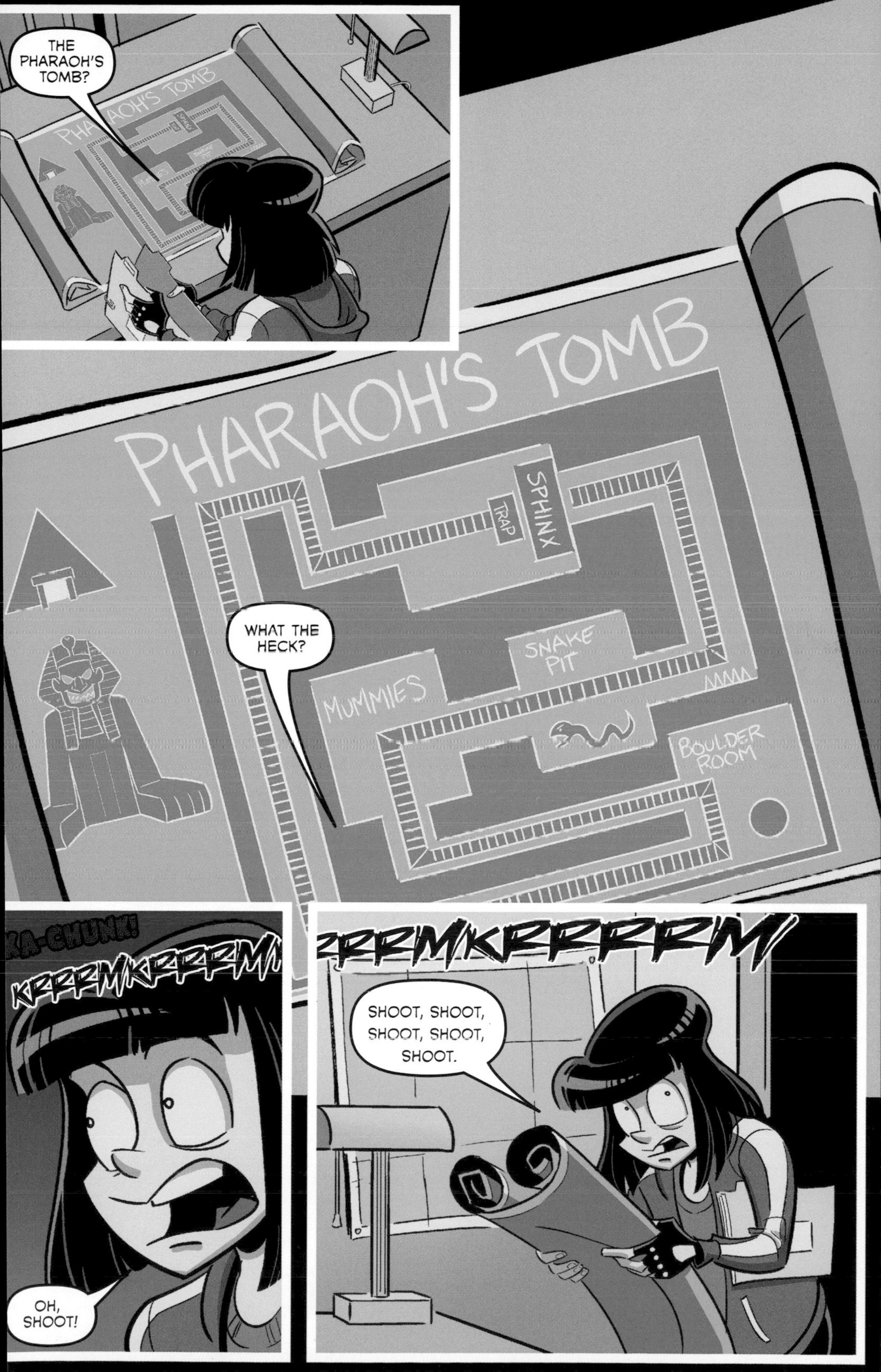

THE PHARAOH'S TOMB?
PHARAOH'S TOMB
PHARAOH'S TOMB
SPHINX
TRAP
WHAT THE HECK?
SNAKE PIT
MUMMIES
BOULDER ROOM
KA-CHUNK!
KRRRMKRRRRM
OH, SHOOT!
RRRMKRRRRRM
SHOOT, SHOOT, SHOOT, SHOOT, SHOOT.

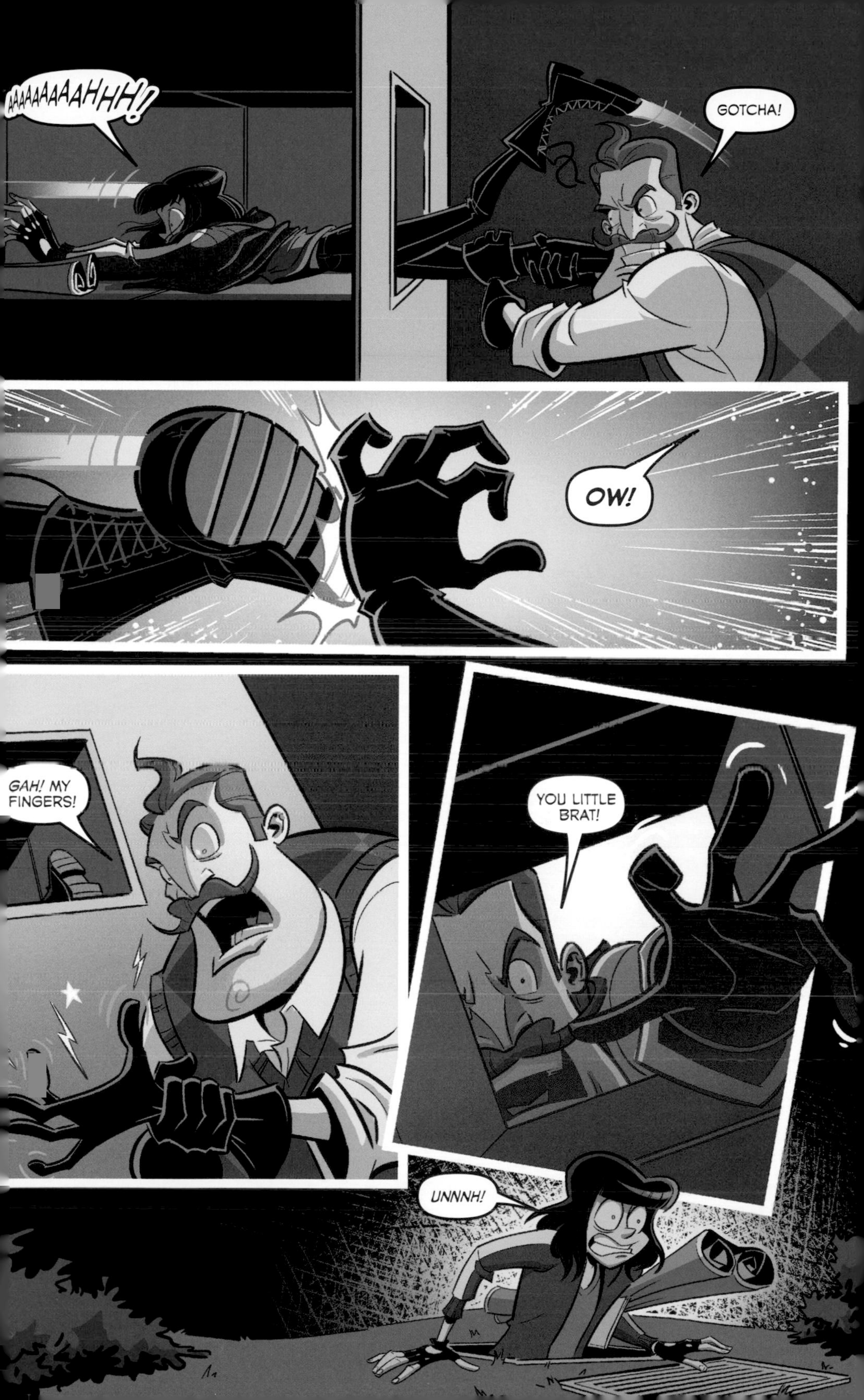
AAAAAAAAAAHHH!!
GOTCHA!
OW!
GAH! MY FINGERS!
YOU LITTLE BRAT!
UNNNH!

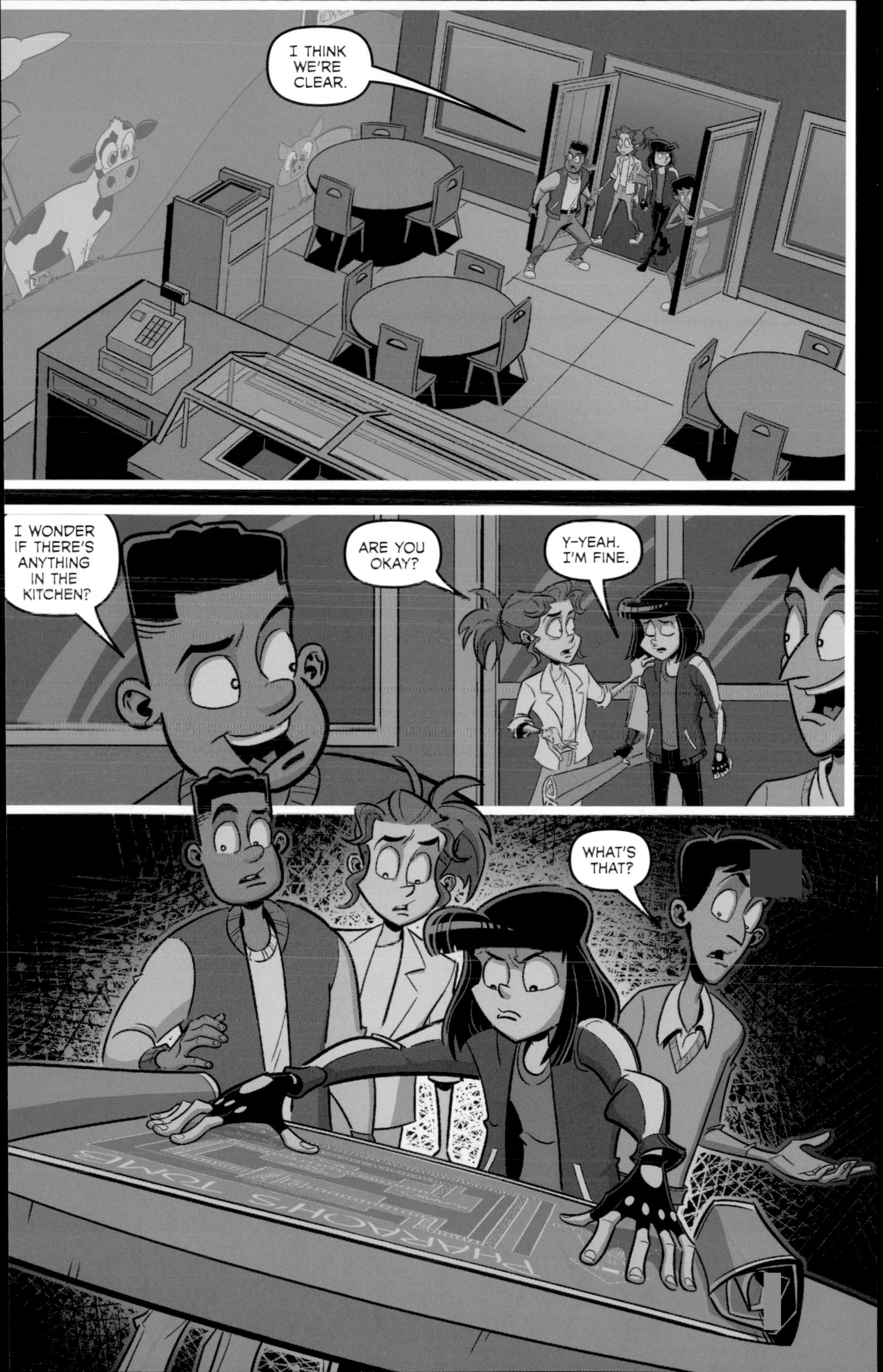
I THINK WE'RE CLEAR.
I WONDER IF THERE'S ANYTHING IN THE KITCHEN?
ARE YOU OKAY?
Y-YEAH. I'M FINE.
WHAT'S THAT?
PHARAOH'S TOMB

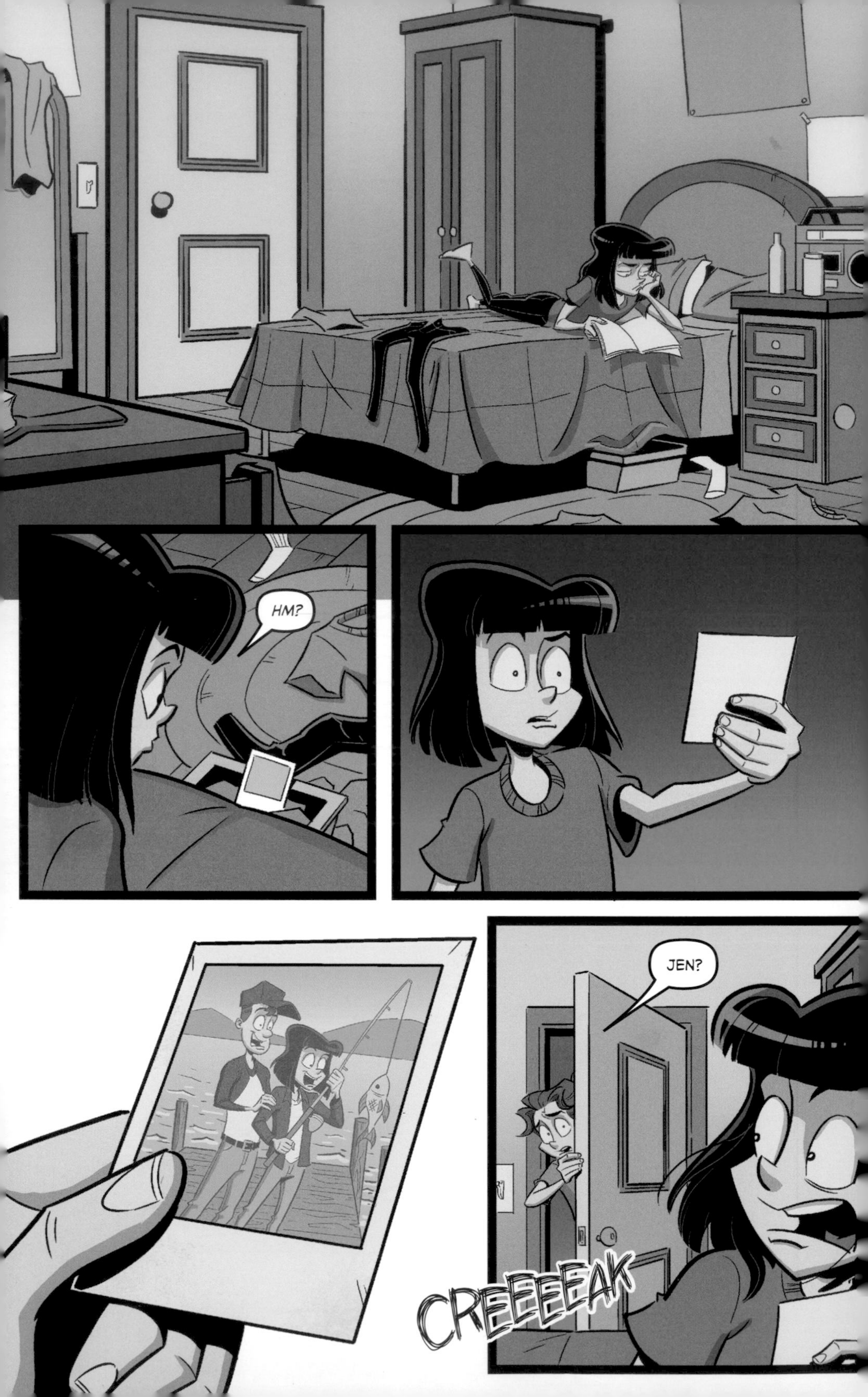
HM?
JEN?
CREEEEEAK

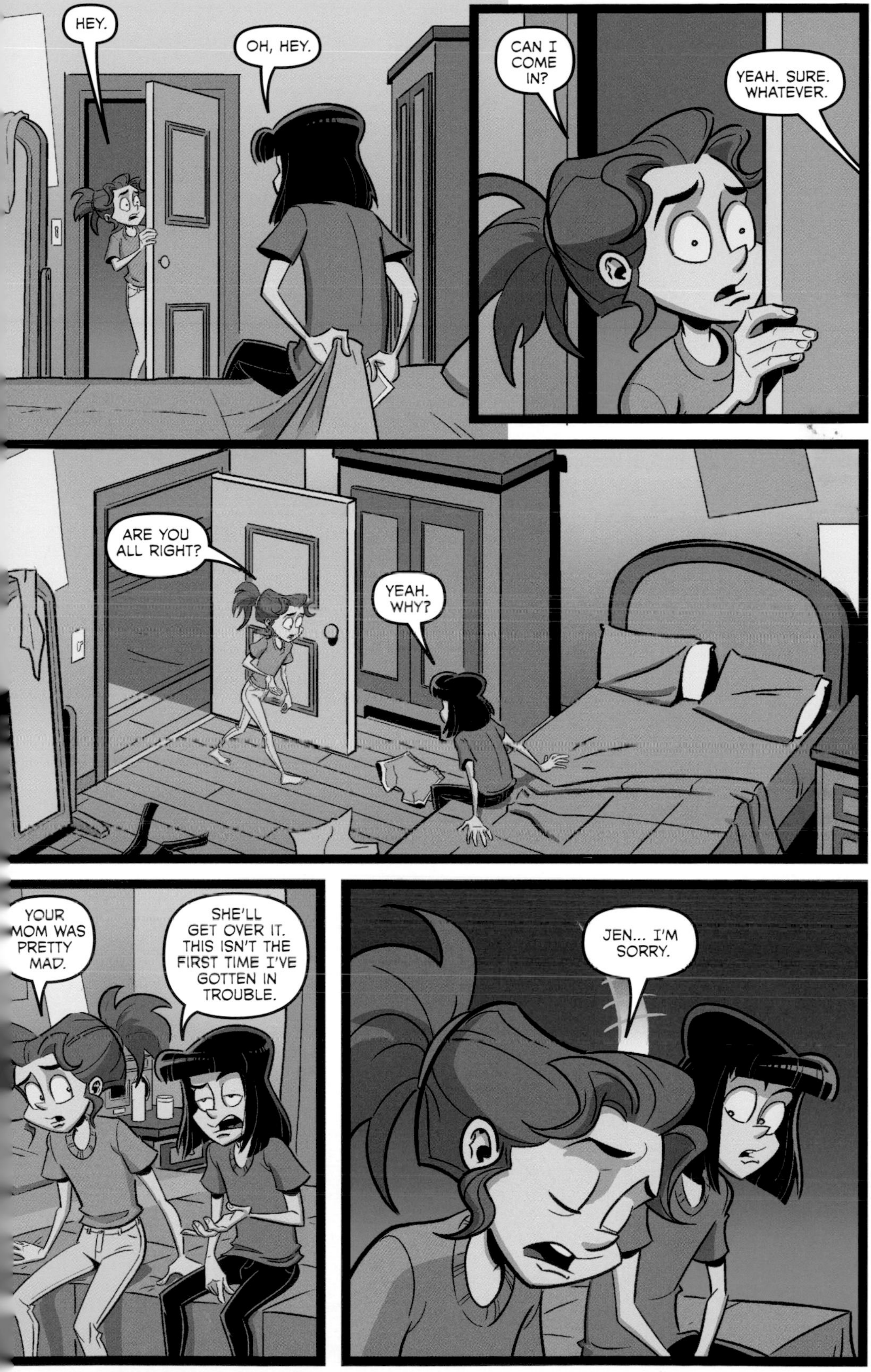
HEY.
OH, HEY.
CAN I COME IN?
YEAH. SURE. WHATEVER.
ARE YOU ALL RIGHT?
YEAH. WHY?
YOUR MOM WAS PRETTY MAD.
SHE'LL GET OVER IT. THIS ISN'T THE FIRST TIME I'VE GOTTEN IN TROUBLE.
JEN... I'M SORRY.

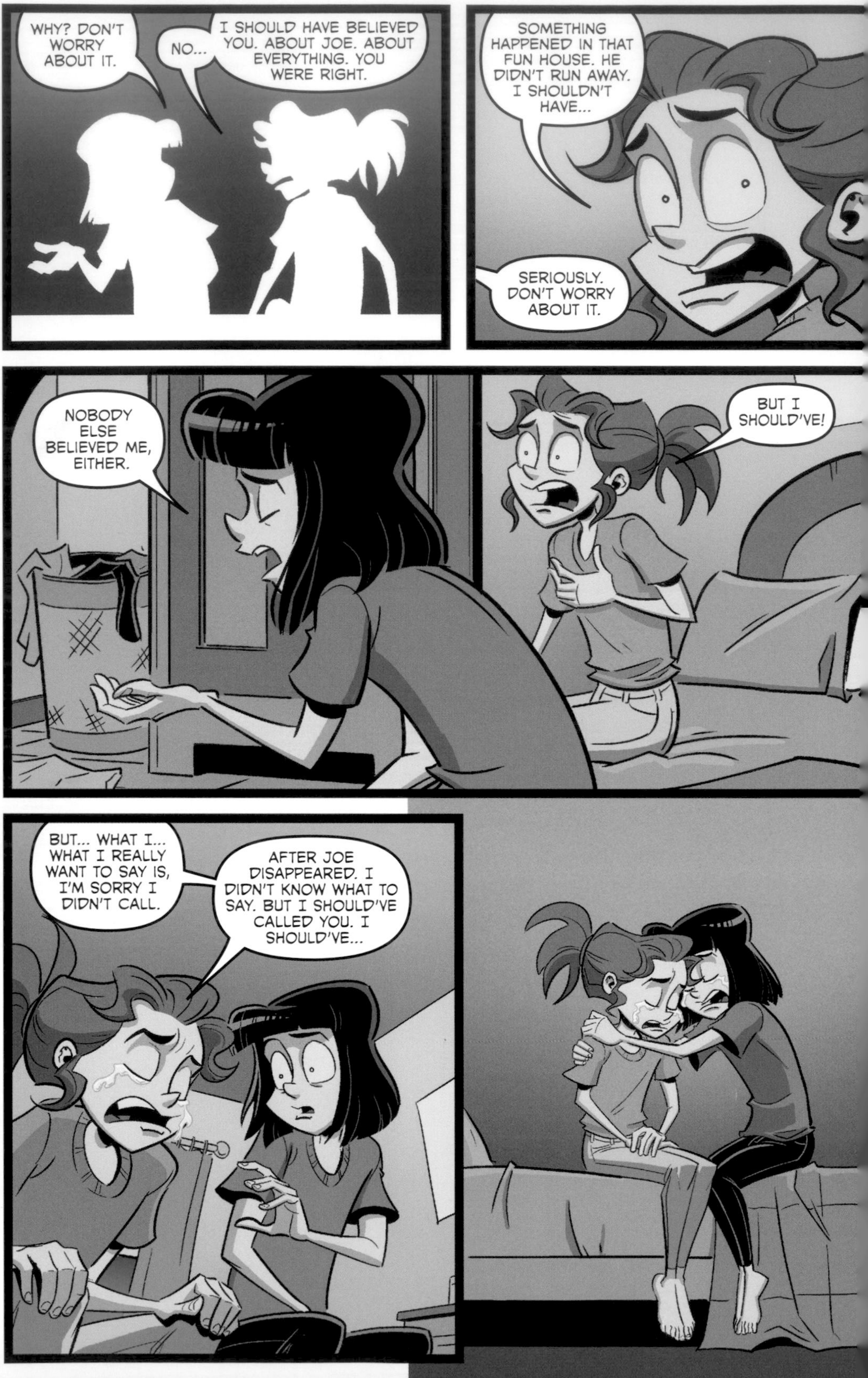

WHY? DON'T WORRY ABOUT IT.
NO...
I SHOULD HAVE BELIEVED YOU. ABOUT JOE. ABOUT EVERYTHING. YOU WERE RIGHT.
SOMETHING HAPPENED IN THAT FUN HOUSE. HE DIDN'T RUN AWAY. I SHOULDN'T HAVE...
SERIOUSLY. DON'T WORRY ABOUT IT.
NOBODY ELSE BELIEVED ME, EITHER.
BUT I SHOULD'VE!
BUT... WHAT I... WHAT I REALLY WANT TO SAY IS, I'M SORRY I DIDN'T CALL.
AFTER JOE DISAPPEARED. I DIDN'T KNOW WHAT TO SAY. BUT I SHOULD'VE CALLED YOU. I SHOULD'VE...

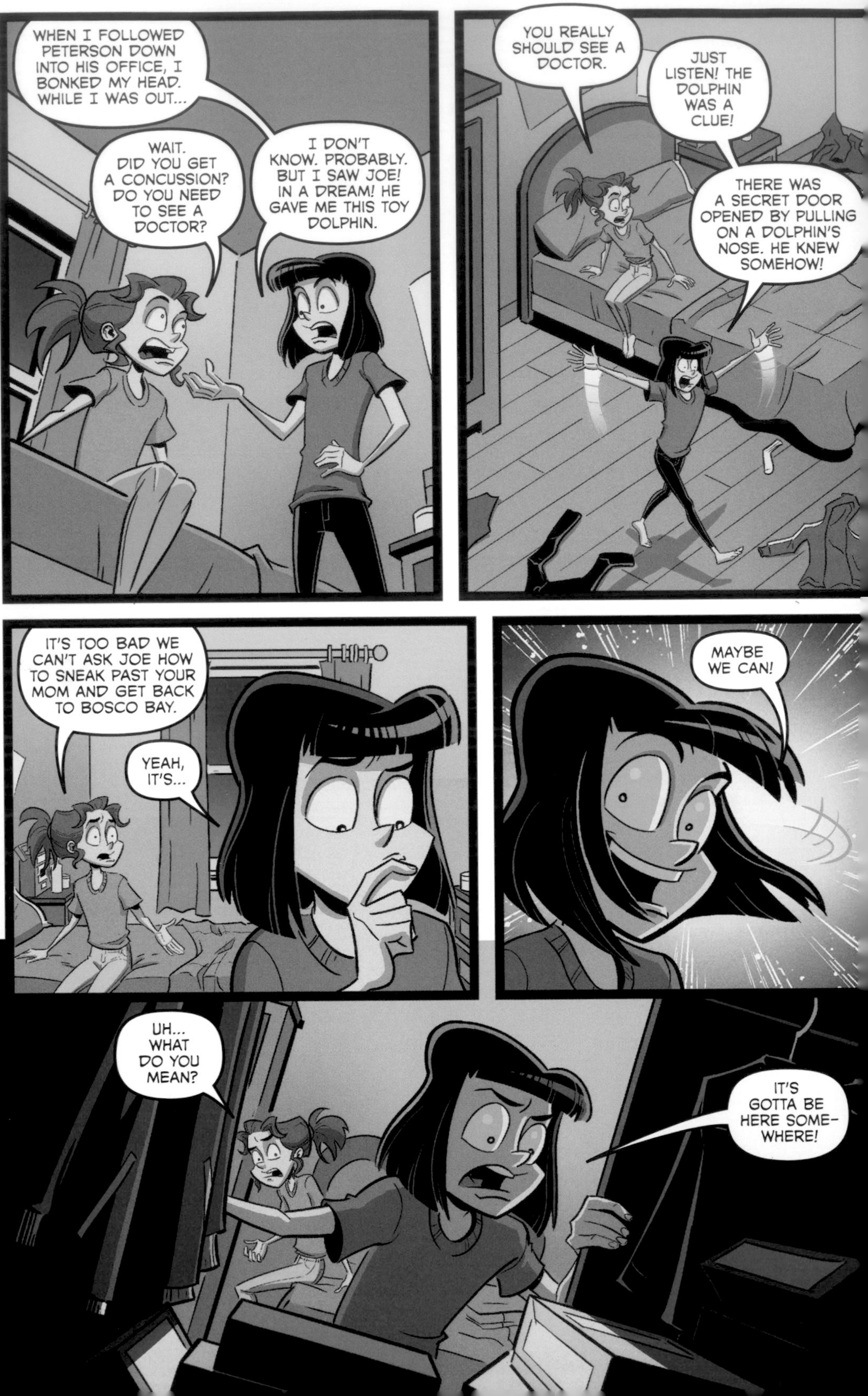
WHEN I FOLLOWED PETERSON DOWN INTO HIS OFFICE, I BONKED MY HEAD. WHILE I WAS OUT...
WAIT. DID YOU GET A CONCUSSION? DO YOU NEED TO SEE A DOCTOR?
I DON'T KNOW. PROBABLY. BUT I SAW JOE! IN A DREAM! HE GAVE ME THIS TOY DOLPHIN.
YOU REALLY SHOULD SEE A DOCTOR.
JUST LISTEN! THE DOLPHIN WAS A CLUE!
THERE WAS A SECRET DOOR OPENED BY PULLING ON A DOLPHIN'S NOSE. HE KNEW SOMEHOW!
IT'S TOO BAD WE CAN'T ASK JOE HOW TO SNEAK PAST YOUR MOM AND GET BACK TO BOSCO BAY.
YEAH, IT'S...
MAYBE WE CAN!
UH... WHAT DO YOU MEAN?
IT'S GOTTA BE HERE SOME-WHERE!

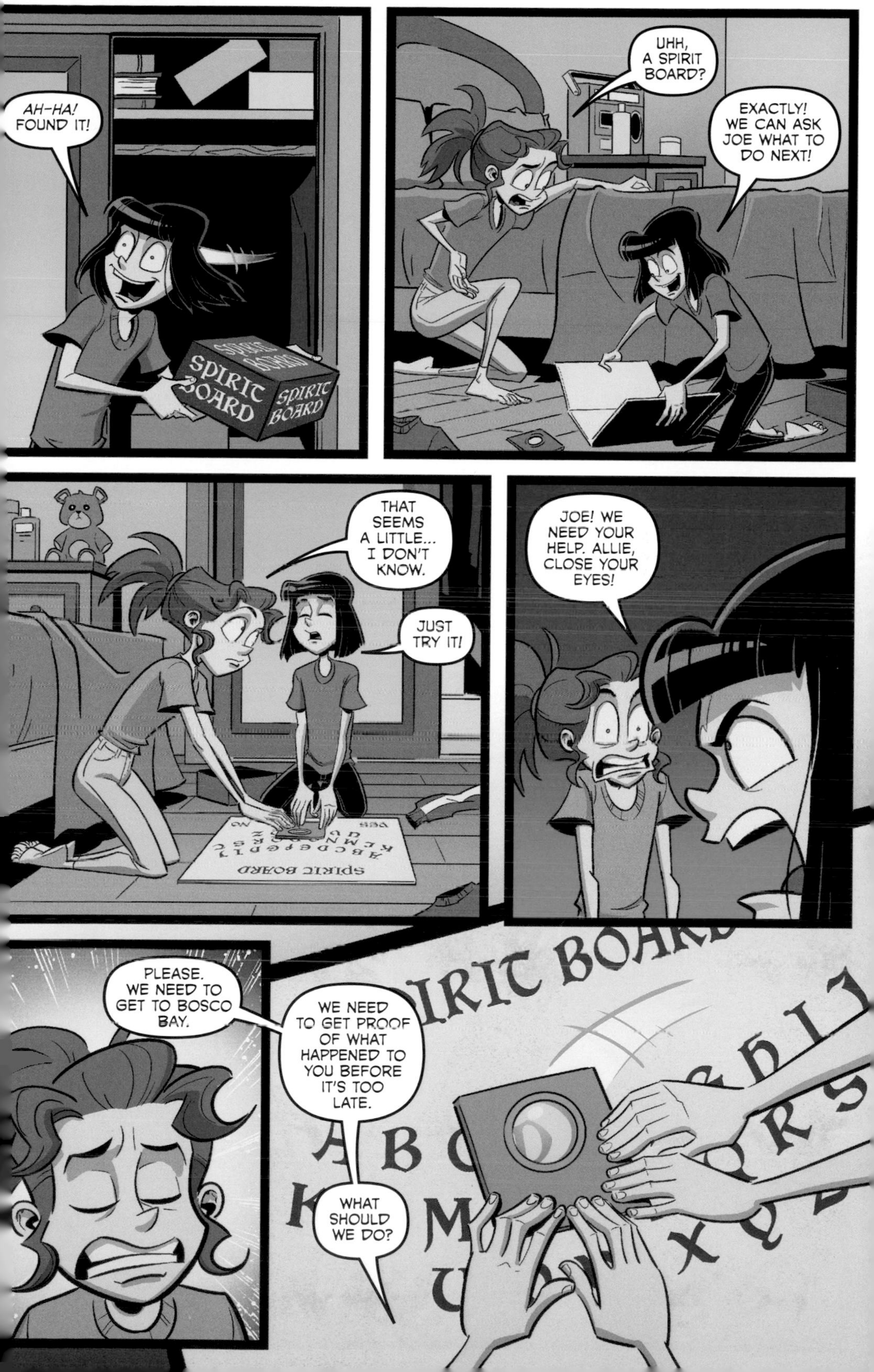
AH-HA! FOUND IT!
SPIRIT BOARD
UHH, A SPIRIT BOARD?
EXACTLY! WE CAN ASK JOE WHAT TO DO NEXT!
THAT SEEMS A LITTLE... I DON'T KNOW.
JUST TRY IT!
JOE! WE NEED YOUR HELP. ALLIE, CLOSE YOUR EYES!
PLEASE. WE NEED TO GET TO BOSCO BAY.
WE NEED TO GET PROOF OF WHAT HAPPENED TO YOU BEFORE IT'S TOO LATE.
WHAT SHOULD WE DO?

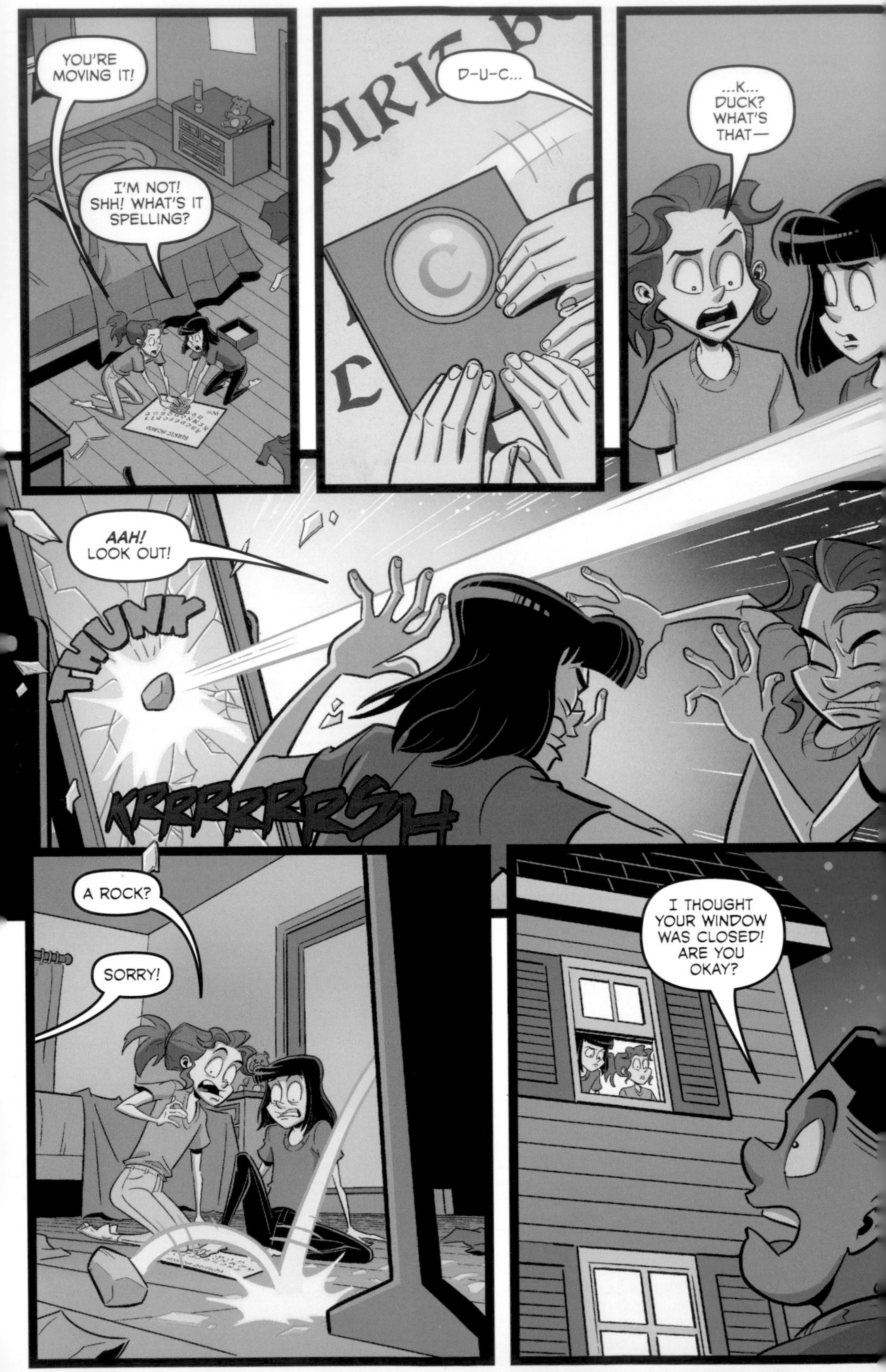

YOU'RE MOVING IT!
I'M NOT! SHH! WHAT'S IT SPELLING?
D-U-C...
...K... DUCK? WHAT'S THAT—
AAH! LOOK OUT!
THUNK
KRRRRRRRSH
A ROCK?
SORRY!
I THOUGHT YOUR WINDOW WAS CLOSED! ARE YOU OKAY?

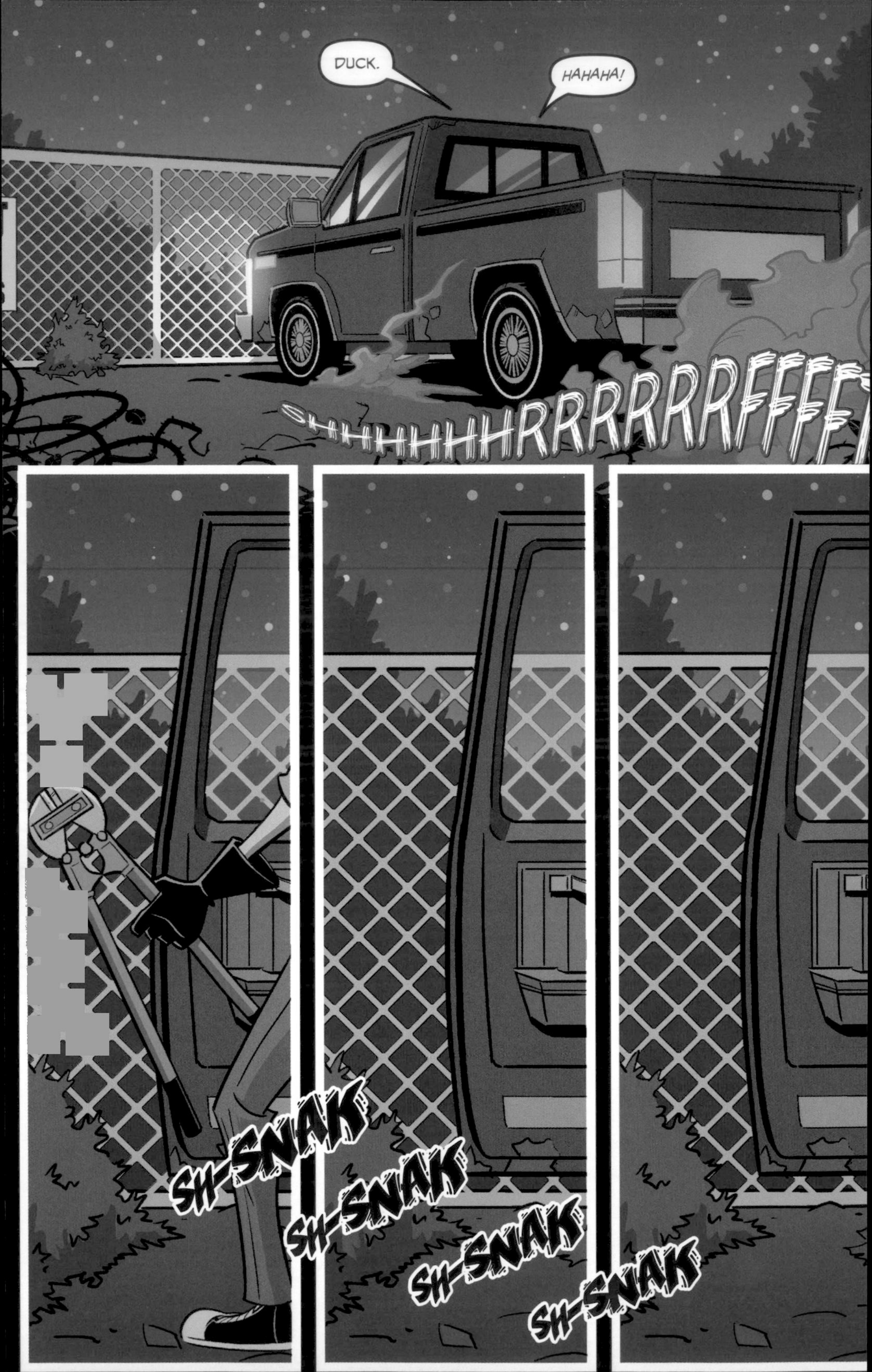
DUCK.
HAHAHA!
SHHHHHHHRRRRRRRFFFFF
SH-SNAK
SH-SNAK
SH-SNAK
SH-SNAK

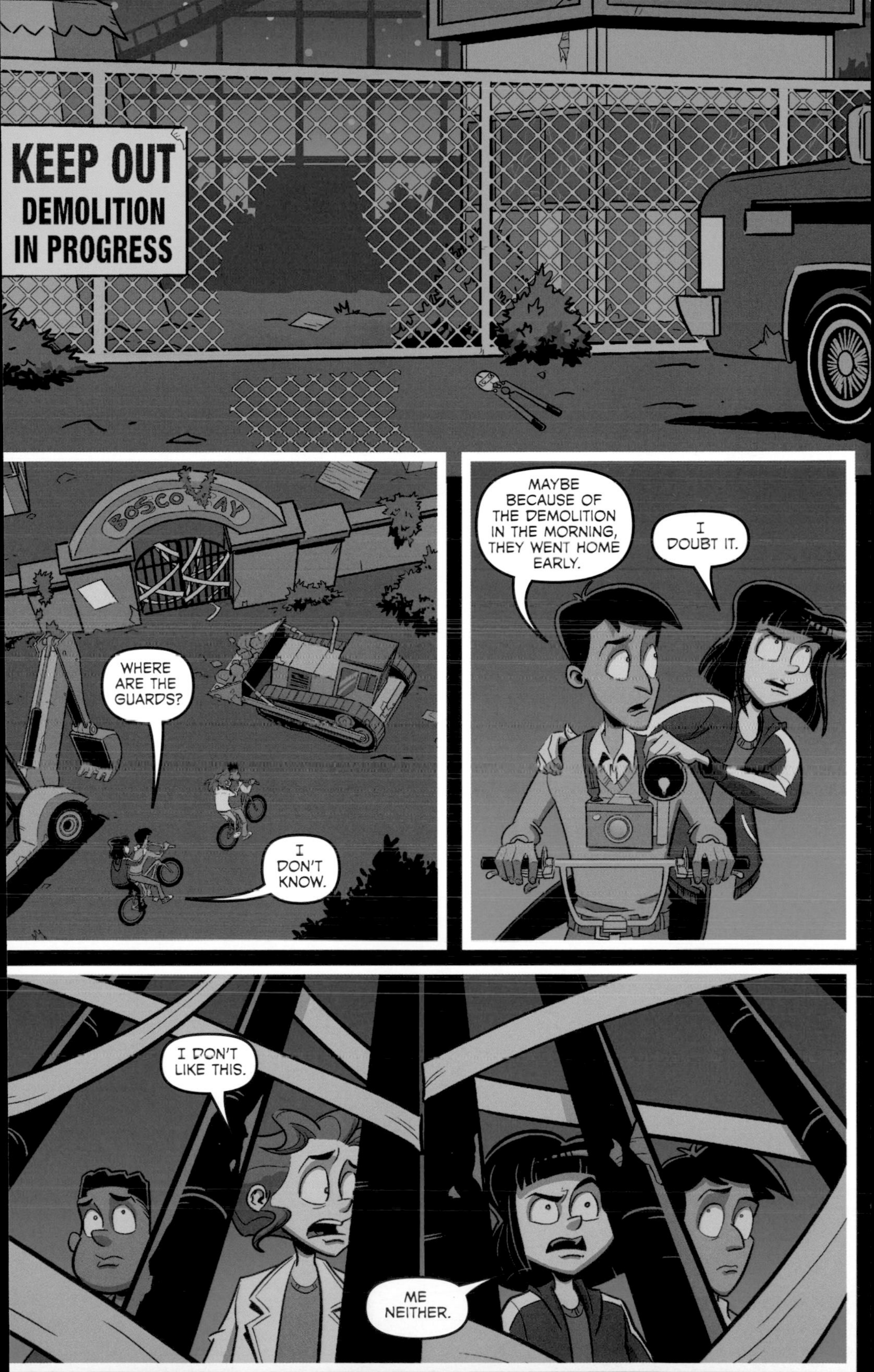
KEEP OUT
DEMOLITION IN PROGRESS
BOSCO BAY
WHERE ARE THE GUARDS?
I DON'T KNOW.
MAYBE BECAUSE OF THE DEMOLITION IN THE MORNING, THEY WENT HOME EARLY.
I DOUBT IT.
I DON'T LIKE THIS.
ME NEITHER.

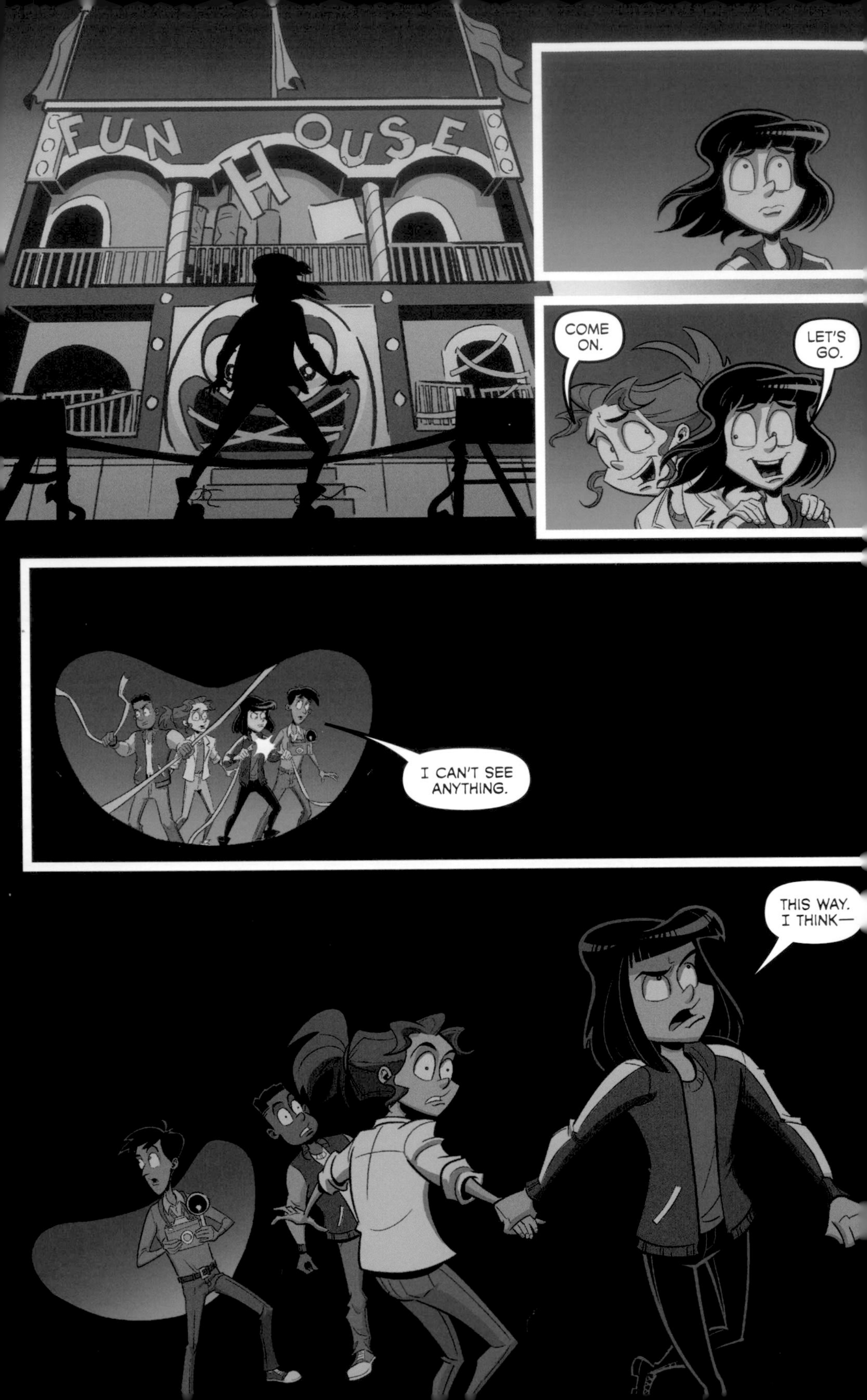
FUN HOUSE
COME ON.
LET'S GO.
I CAN'T SEE ANYTHING.
THIS WAY. I THINK—

OH NO.

HOLD ON!

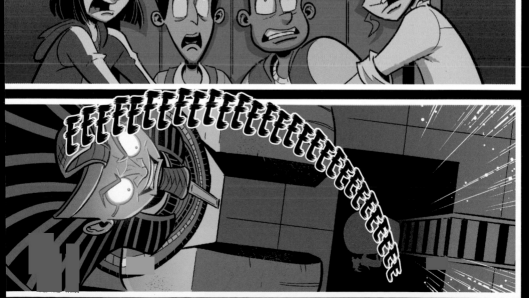

EEEEEEEEEEEEEEEEEEEEEEEEEEEEEEEEEE

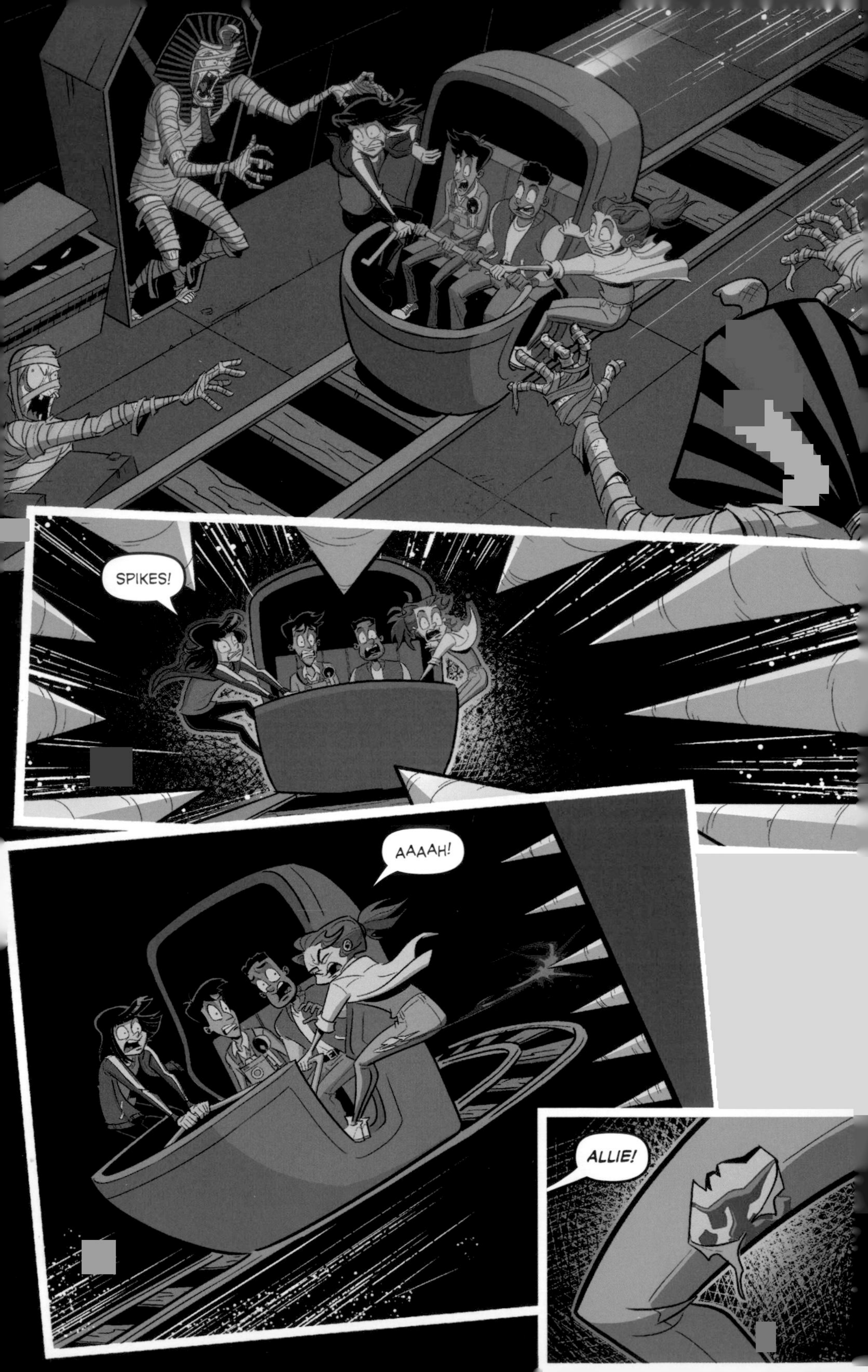
SPIKES!
AAAAH!
ALLIE!

JEN? ARE YOU?

KLIK-VREEEE

KLIK-VREEEE

JEN. IT'S OKAY.

NO. IT'S NOT.

BUT IT WILL BE. AS SOON AS I GET THESE PICTURES TO THE POLICE.

IS THAT SO?

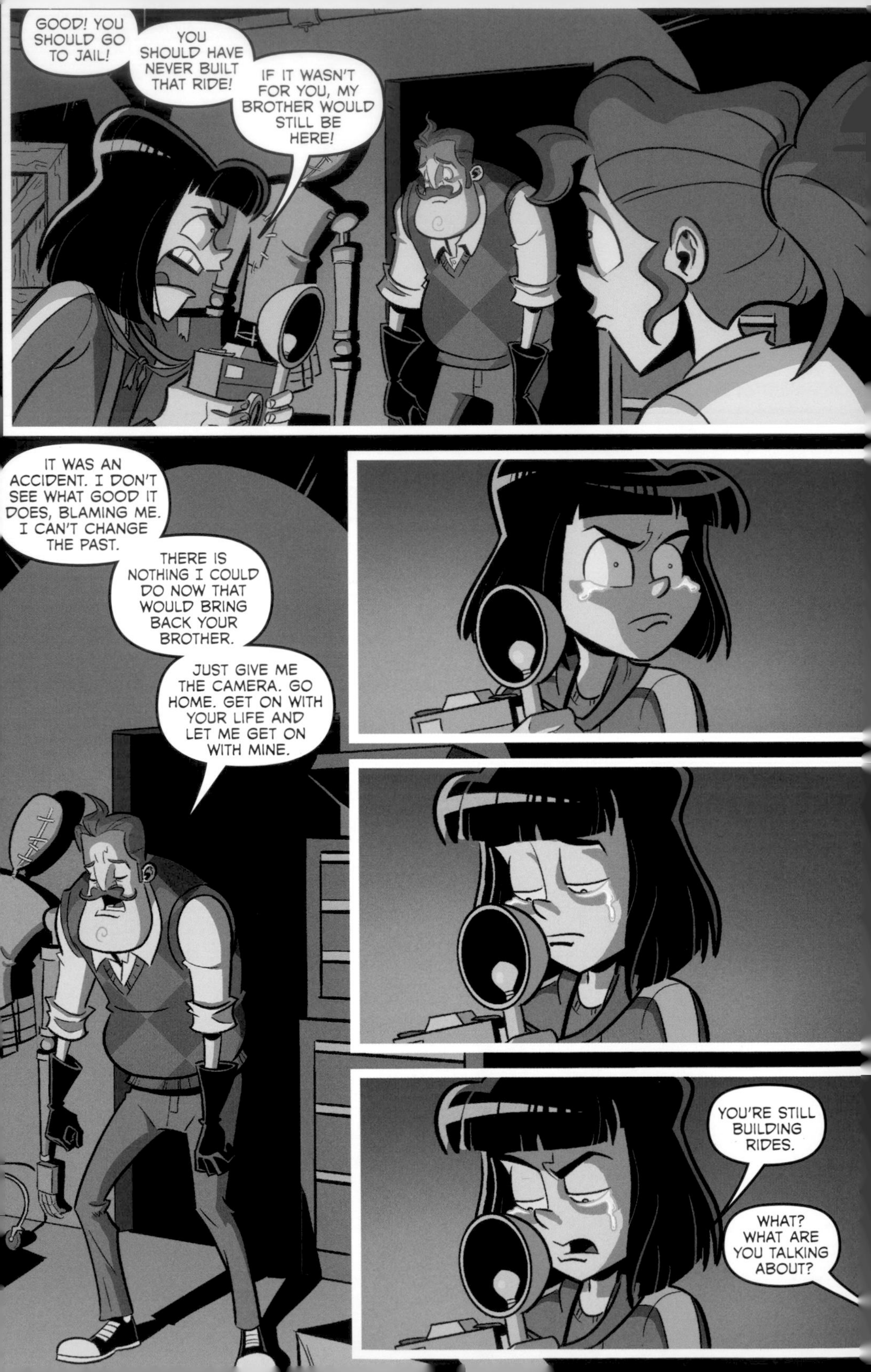
GOOD! YOU SHOULD GO TO JAIL!
YOU SHOULD HAVE NEVER BUILT THAT RIDE!
IF IT WASN'T FOR YOU, MY BROTHER WOULD STILL BE HERE!
IT WAS AN ACCIDENT. I DON'T SEE WHAT GOOD IT DOES, BLAMING ME. I CAN'T CHANGE THE PAST.
THERE IS NOTHING I COULD DO NOW THAT WOULD BRING BACK YOUR BROTHER.
JUST GIVE ME THE CAMERA. GO HOME. GET ON WITH YOUR LIFE AND LET ME GET ON WITH MINE.
YOU'RE STILL BUILDING RIDES.
WHAT? WHAT ARE YOU TALKING ABOUT?

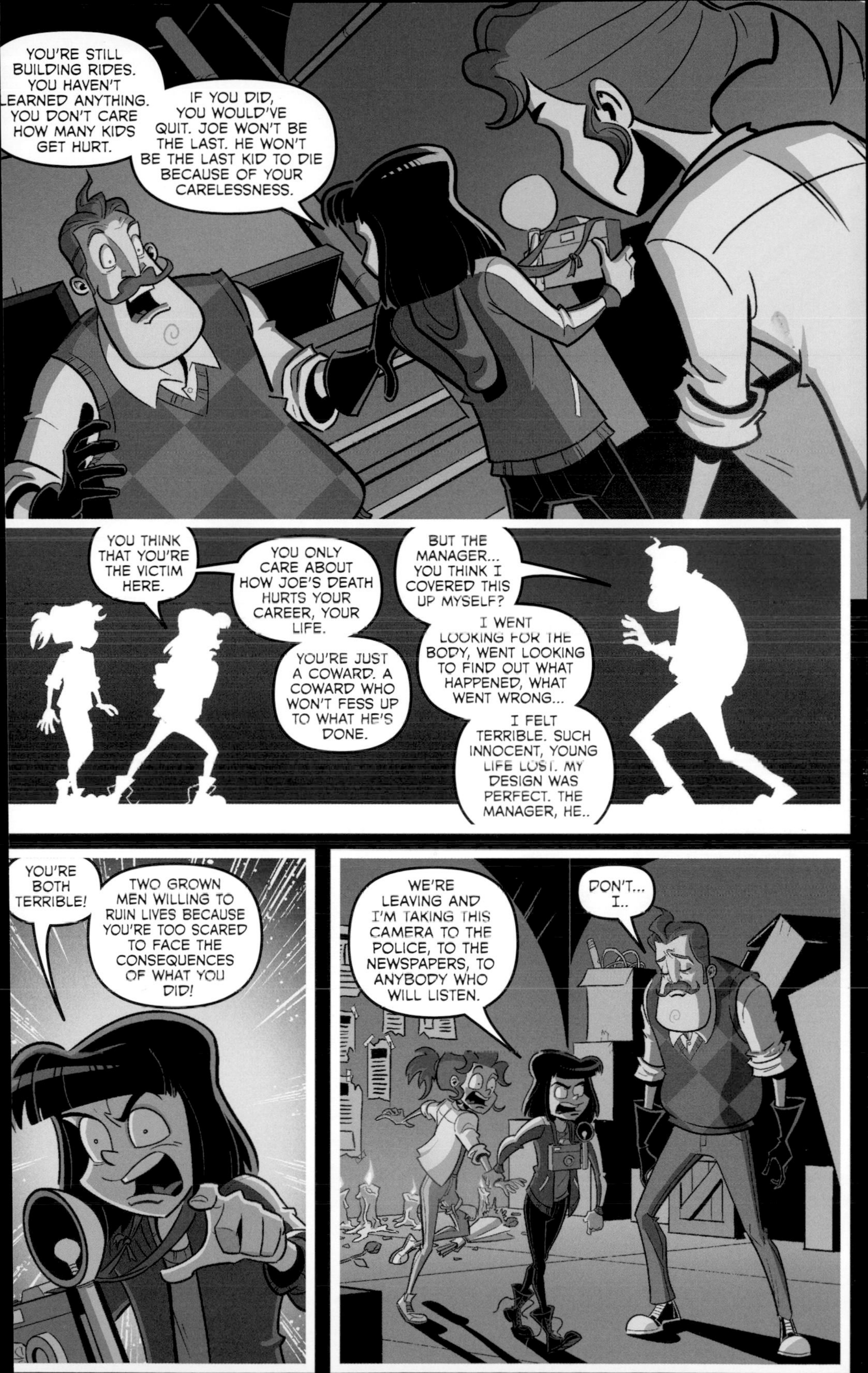
YOU'RE STILL BUILDING RIDES. YOU HAVEN'T LEARNED ANYTHING. YOU DON'T CARE HOW MANY KIDS GET HURT.
IF YOU DID, YOU WOULD'VE QUIT. JOE WON'T BE THE LAST. HE WON'T BE THE LAST KID TO DIE BECAUSE OF YOUR CARELESSNESS.
YOU THINK THAT YOU'RE THE VICTIM HERE.
YOU ONLY CARE ABOUT HOW JOE'S DEATH HURTS YOUR CAREER, YOUR LIFE.
YOU'RE JUST A COWARD. A COWARD WHO WON'T FESS UP TO WHAT HE'S DONE.
BUT THE MANAGER... YOU THINK I COVERED THIS UP MYSELF?
I WENT LOOKING FOR THE BODY, WENT LOOKING TO FIND OUT WHAT HAPPENED, WHAT WENT WRONG...
I FELT TERRIBLE. SUCH INNOCENT, YOUNG LIFE LOST. MY DESIGN WAS PERFECT. THE MANAGER, HE..
YOU'RE BOTH TERRIBLE!
TWO GROWN MEN WILLING TO RUIN LIVES BECAUSE YOU'RE TOO SCARED TO FACE THE CONSEQUENCES OF WHAT YOU DID!
WE'RE LEAVING AND I'M TAKING THIS CAMERA TO THE POLICE, TO THE NEWSPAPERS, TO ANYBODY WHO WILL LISTEN.
DON'T... I..

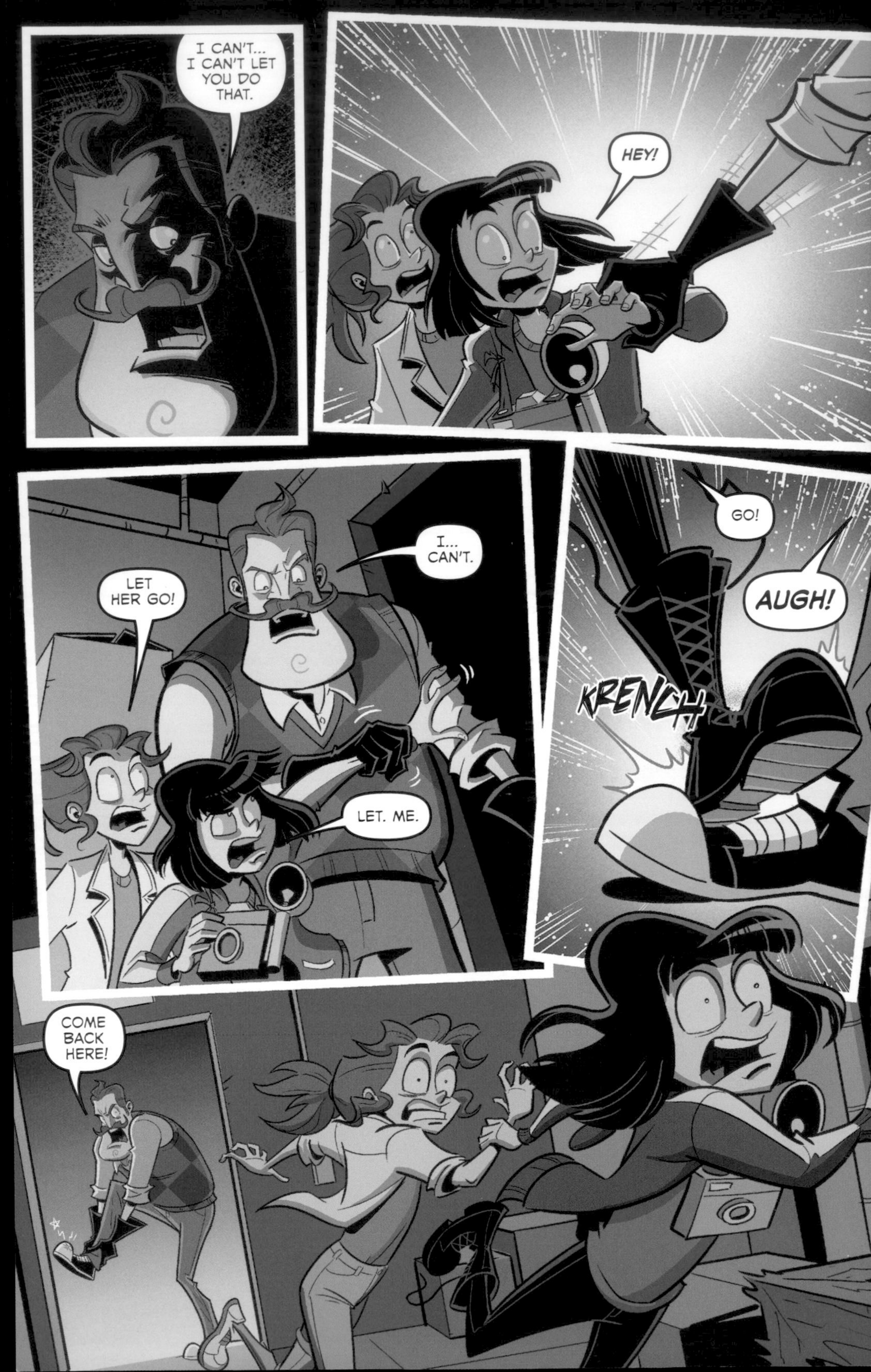
I CAN'T... I CAN'T LET YOU DO THAT.
HEY!
LET HER GO!
I... CAN'T.
LET. ME.
GO!
AUGH!
KRENCH
COME BACK HERE!

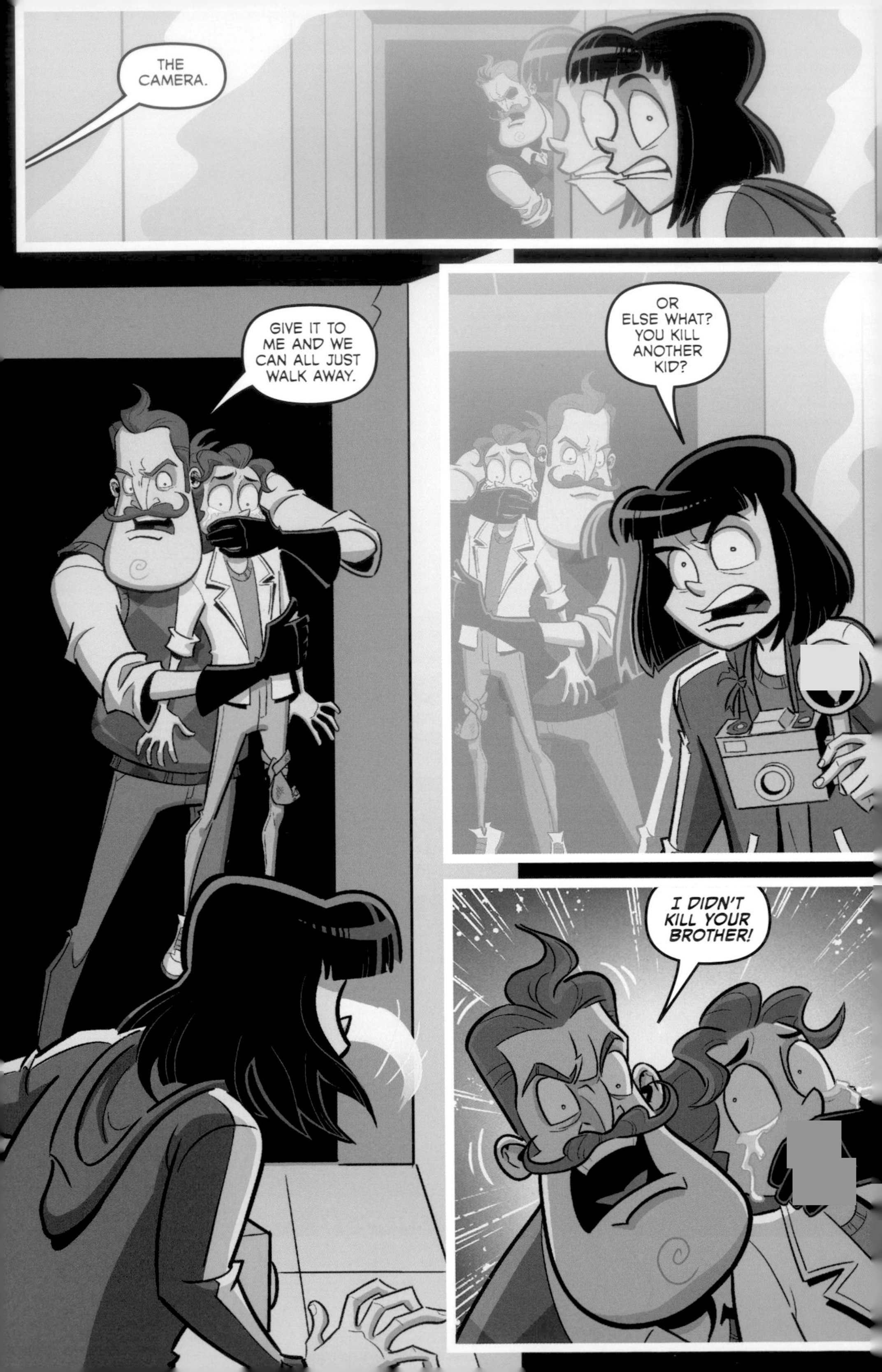
THE CAMERA.
GIVE IT TO ME AND WE CAN ALL JUST WALK AWAY.
OR ELSE WHAT? YOU KILL ANOTHER KID?
I DIDN'T KILL YOUR BROTHER!

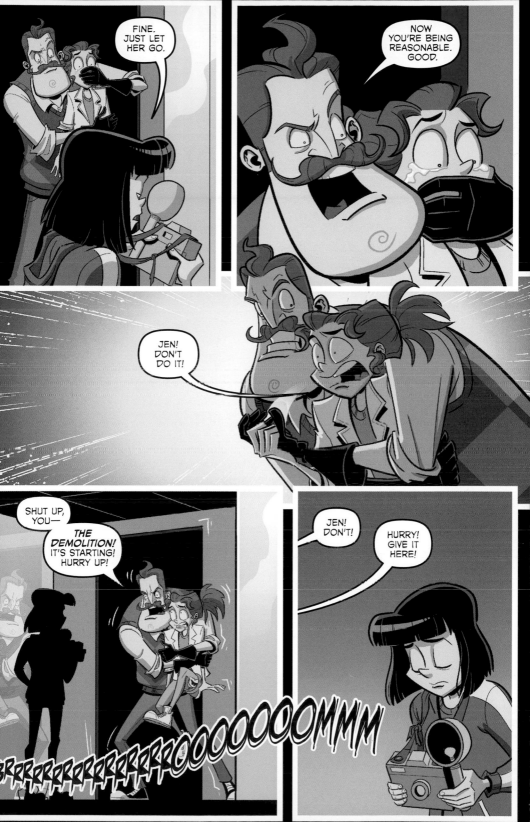

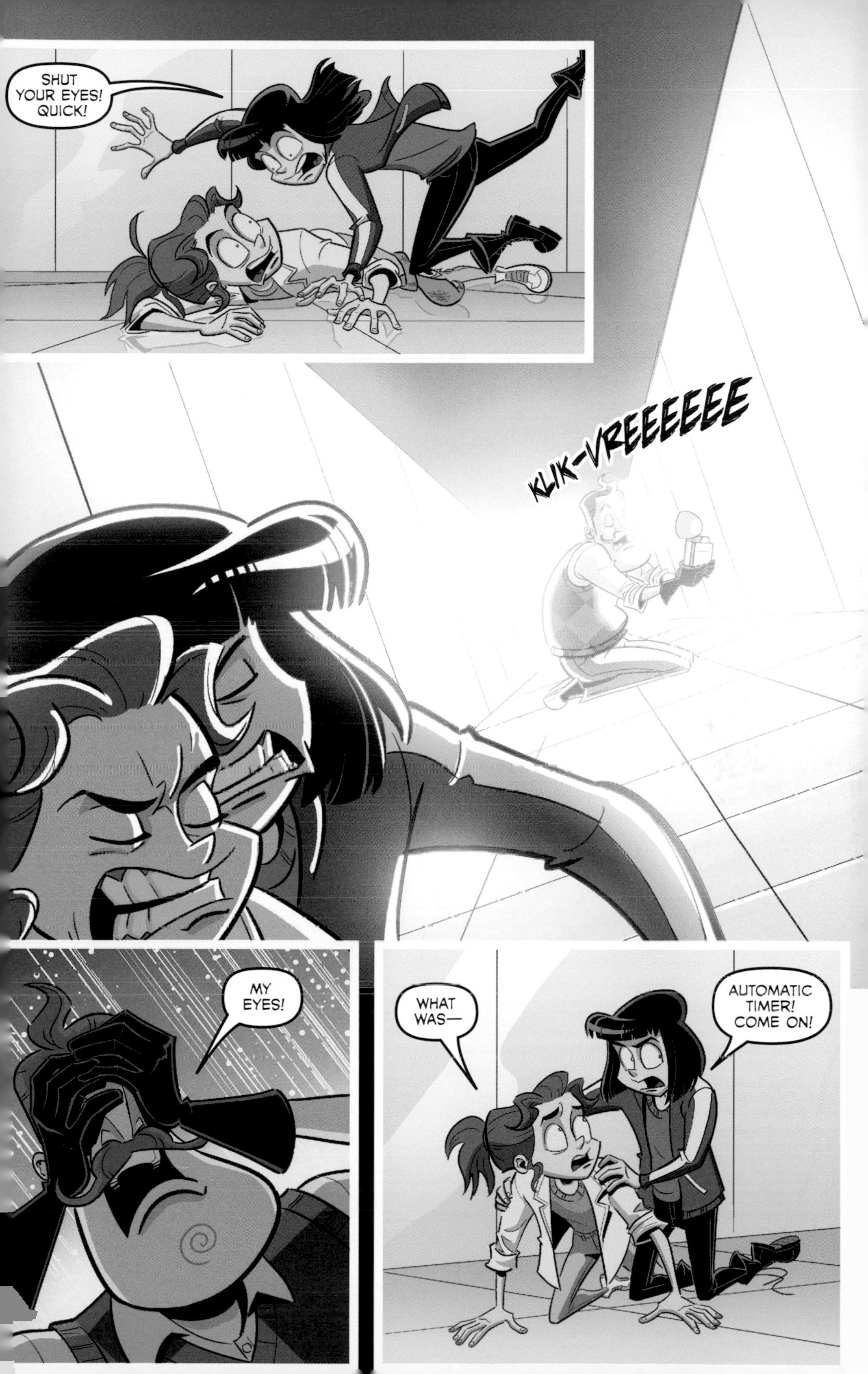
SHUT YOUR EYES! QUICK!
KLIK-VREEEEEEE
MY EYES!
WHAT WAS—
AUTOMATIC TIMER! COME ON!

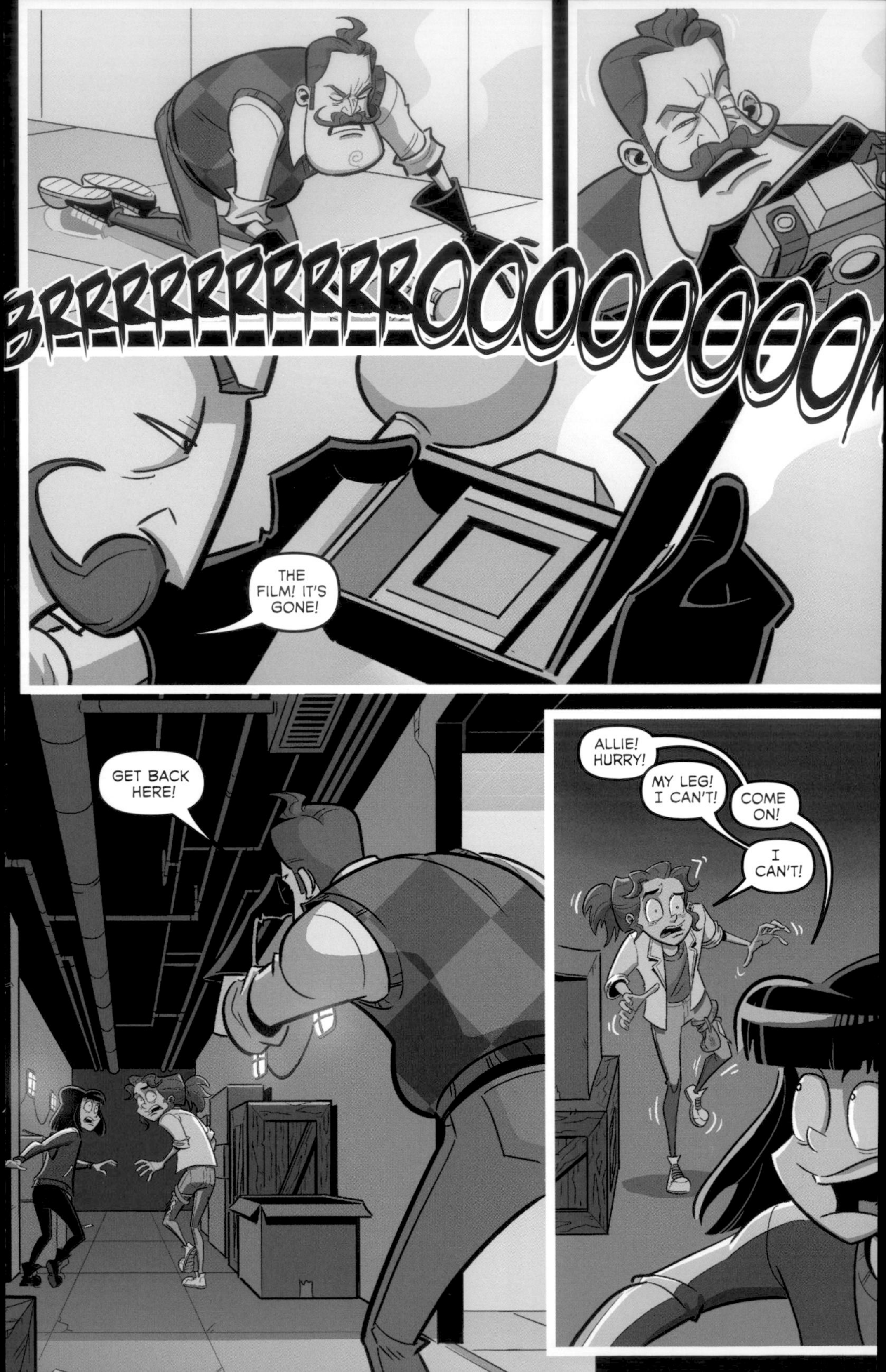
BRRRRRRRRRRRROOOOOOOOOOM!
THE FILM! IT'S GONE!
GET BACK HERE!
ALLIE! HURRY!
MY LEG! I CAN'T!
COME ON!
I CAN'T!

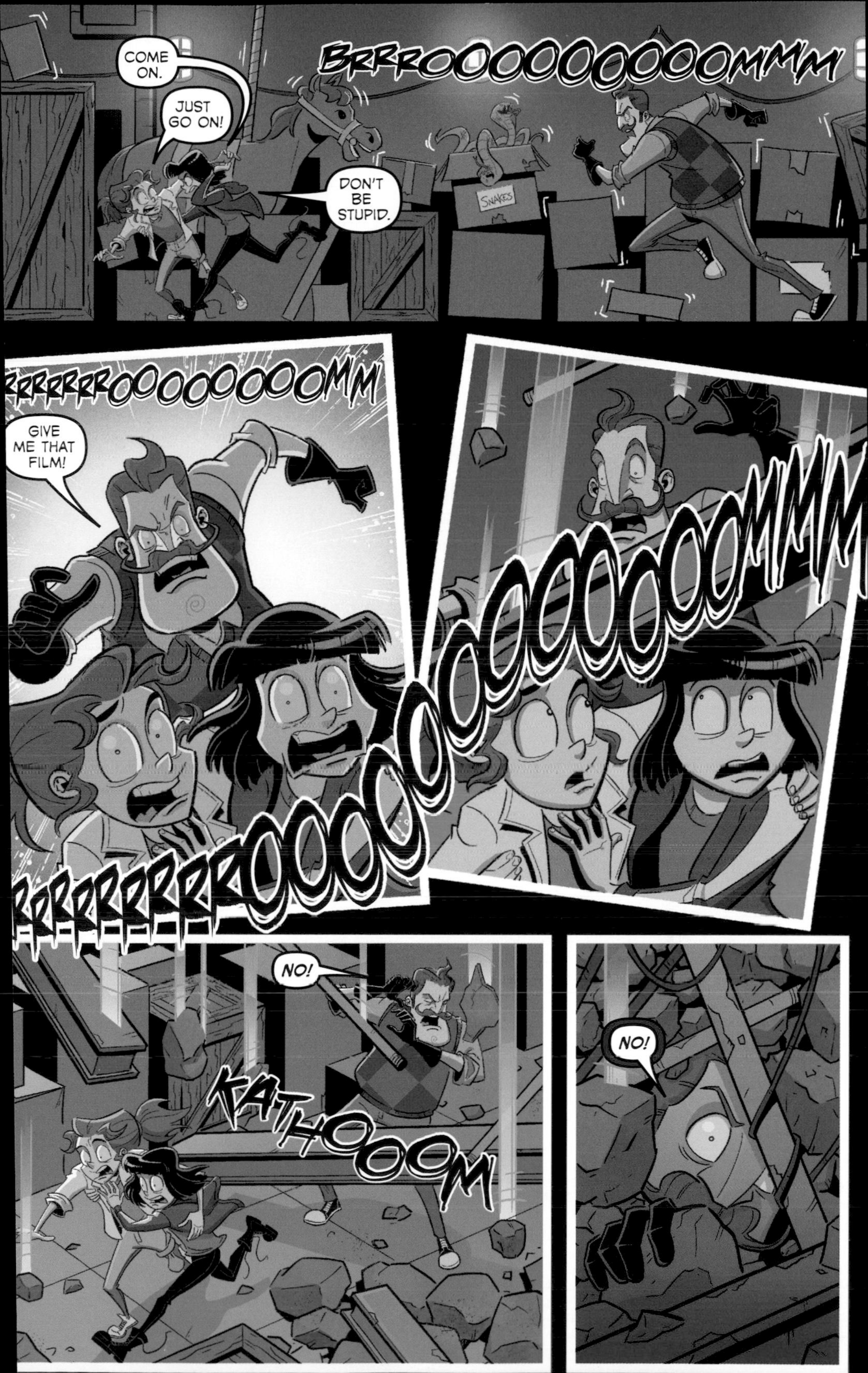
COME ON.
JUST GO ON!
BRRROOOOOOOOOOMMM
DON'T BE STUPID.
RRRRRRROOOOOOOOOMM
GIVE ME THAT FILM!
RRRRRRRRROOOOOOOOOOOOOOOOOOOMMM
NO!
KATHOOOM
NO!

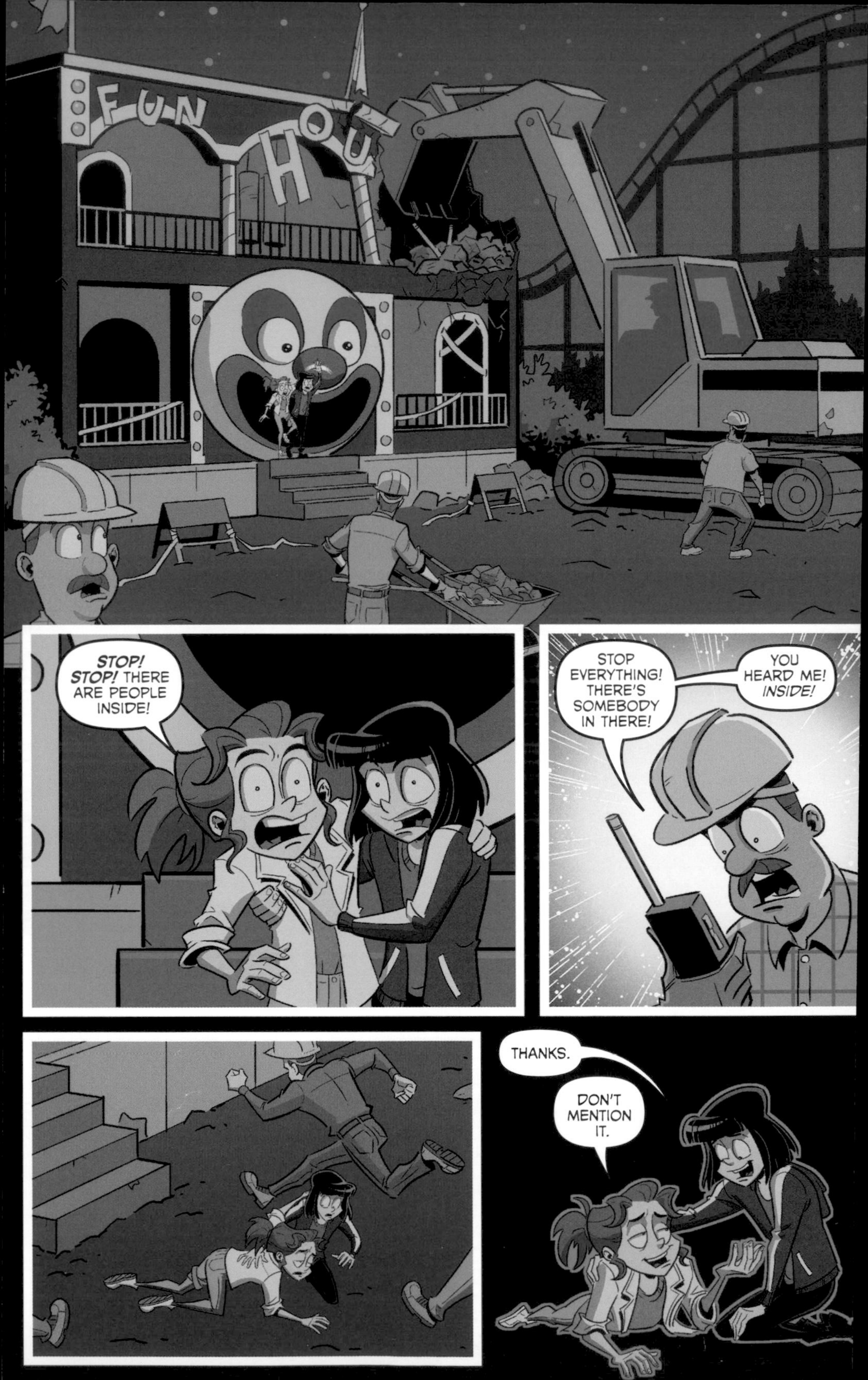
FUN HOU
STOP! STOP! THERE ARE PEOPLE INSIDE!
STOP EVERYTHING! THERE'S SOMEBODY IN THERE!
YOU HEARD ME! INSIDE!
THANKS.
DON'T MENTION IT.

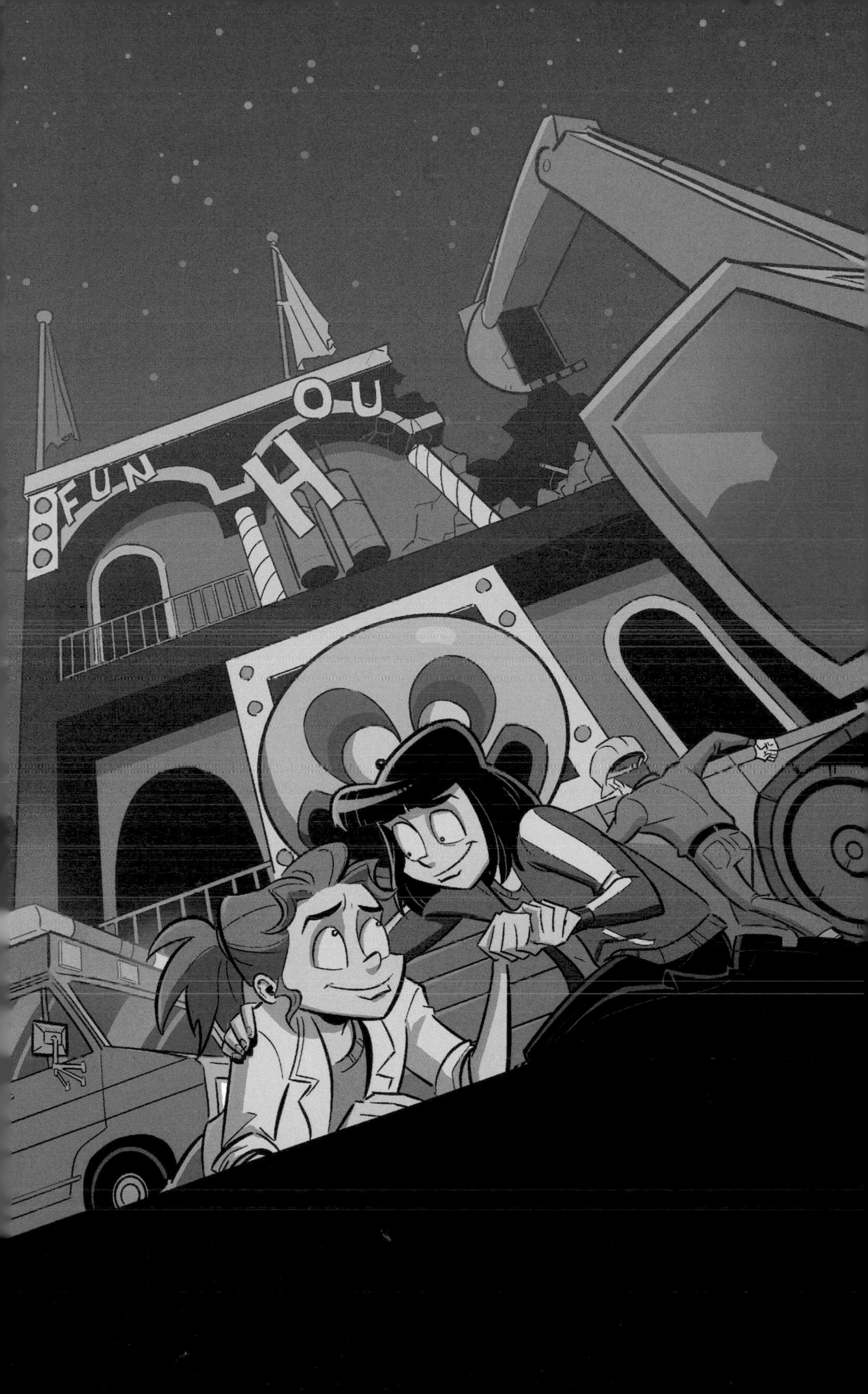
FUN

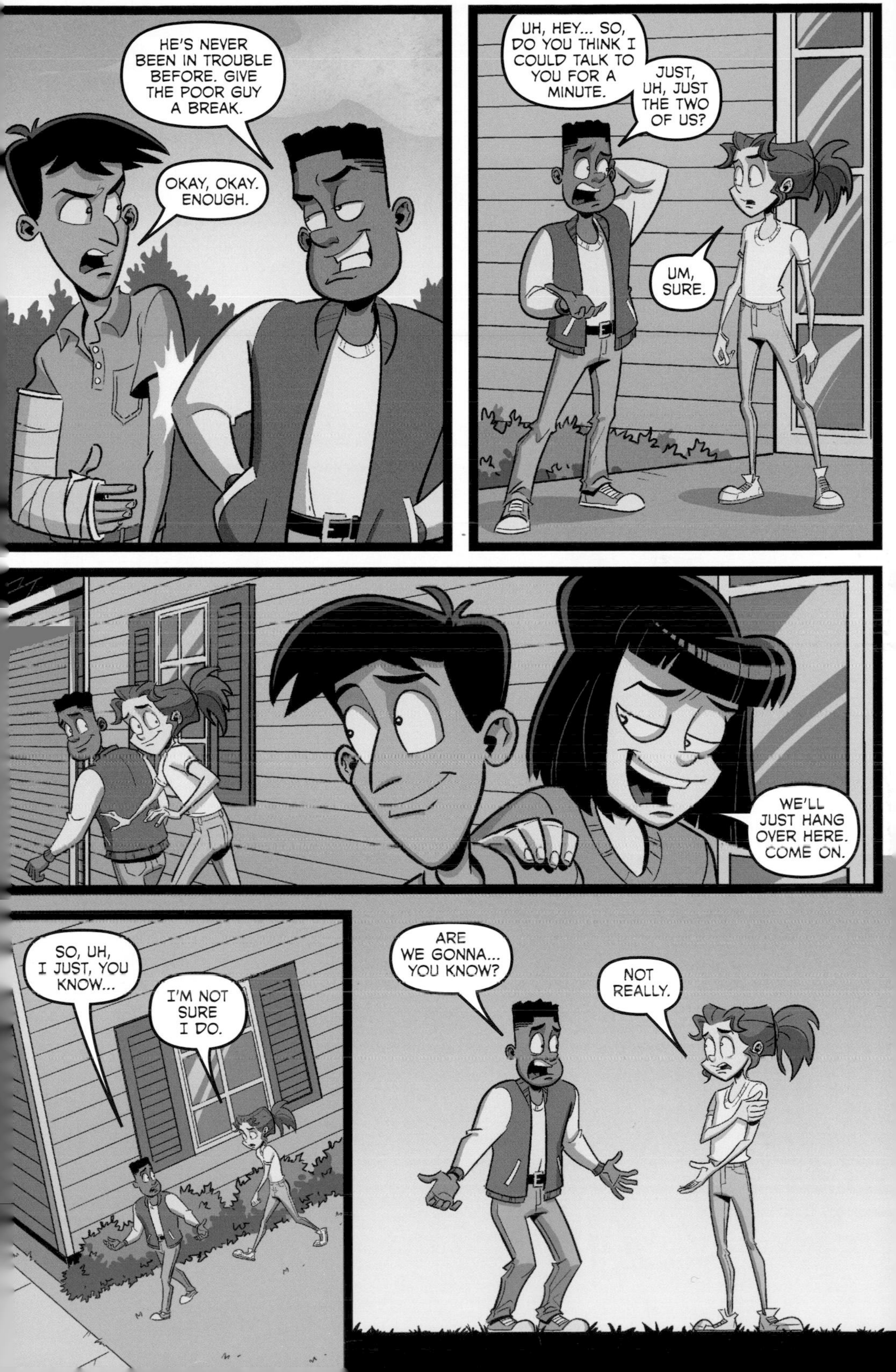
HE'S NEVER BEEN IN TROUBLE BEFORE. GIVE THE POOR GUY A BREAK.
OKAY, OKAY. ENOUGH.
UH, HEY... SO, DO YOU THINK I COULD TALK TO YOU FOR A MINUTE.
JUST, UH, JUST THE TWO OF US?
UM, SURE.
WE'LL JUST HANG OVER HERE. COME ON.
SO, UH, I JUST, YOU KNOW...
I'M NOT SURE I DO.
ARE WE GONNA... YOU KNOW?
NOT REALLY.

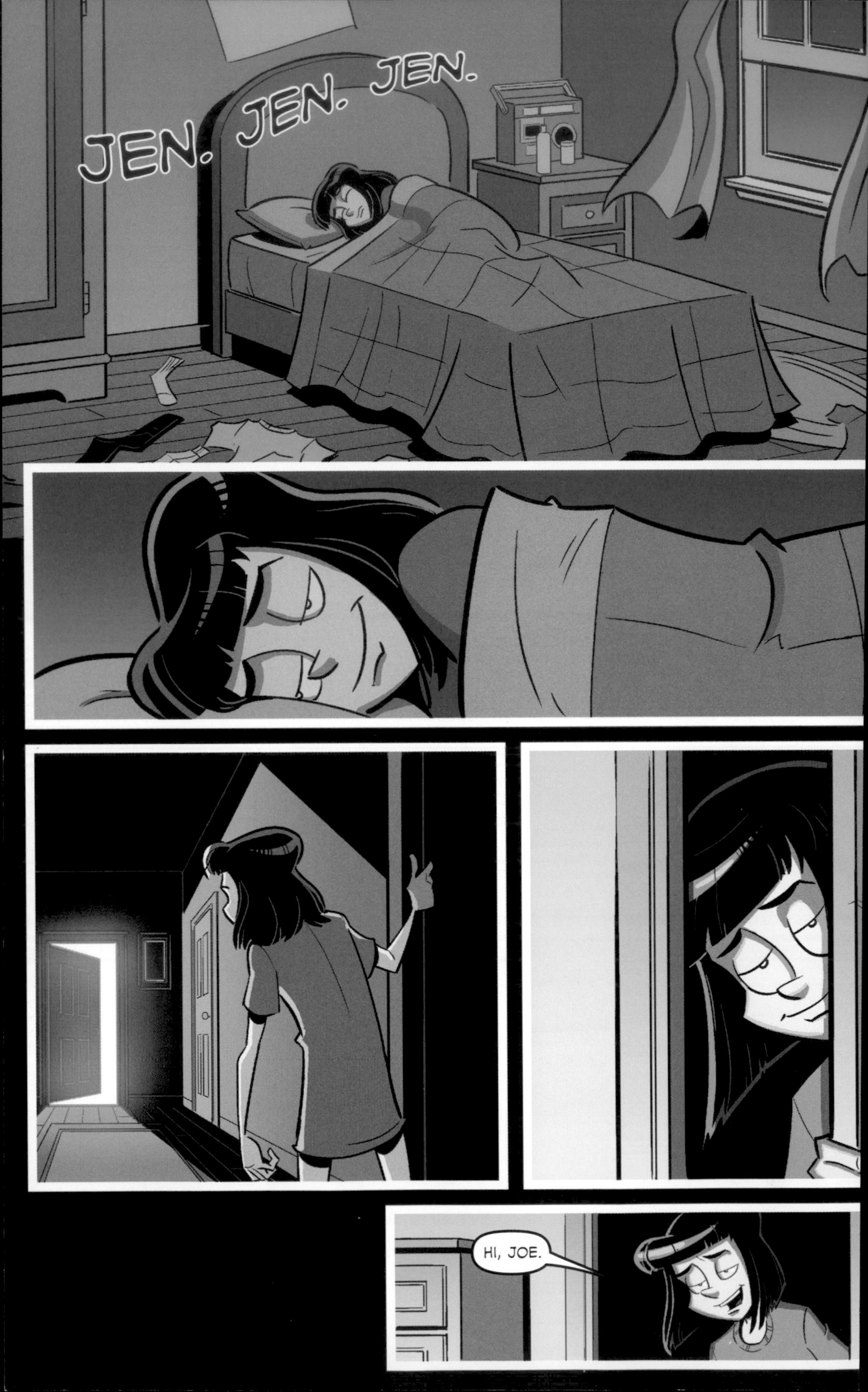
JEN. JEN. JEN.
HI, JOE.

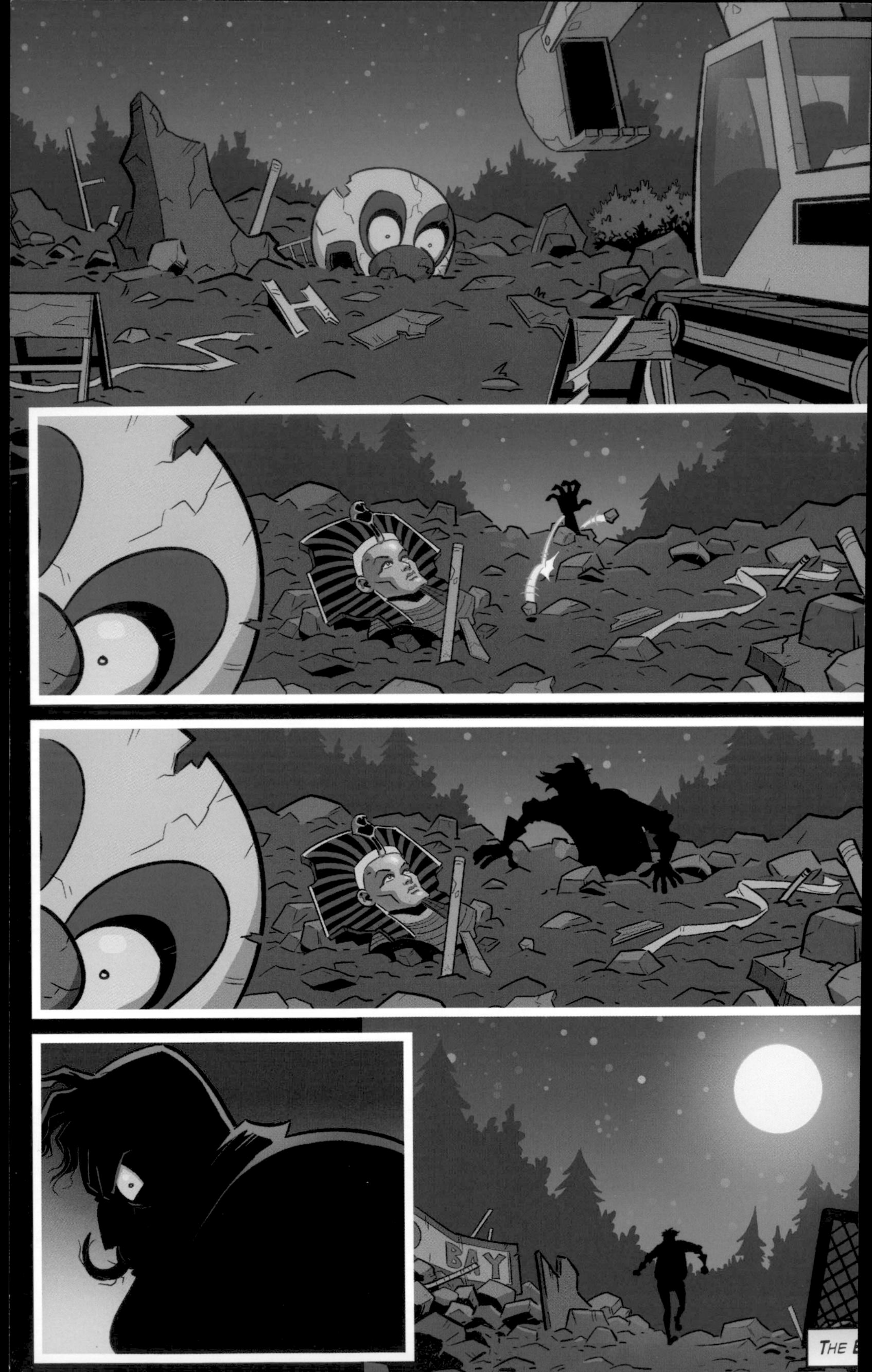
BAY
THE